DOCTOR'S SECRET TWINS
AN AGE GAP ROMANCE

CRYSTAL MONROE

Copyright © 2023 by Crystal Monroe

All rights reserved.

No part of this book may be reproduced in any form or by any electronic or mechanical means, including information storage and retrieval systems, without written permission from the author, except for the use of brief quotations in a book review.

Cover Artwork © 2023 L.J. Anderson of Mayhem Cover Creations

DESCRIPTION

My doctor just told me I'm pregnant...
With HIS babies.

Luke's the one-night stand I can't quit.
An arrogant prick in a mouth-watering package.

I swore I was done with his trance-inducing blue eyes and smug lectures.
Then he moves next door.
Now that we're neighbors, I can't resist his... *manual dexterity*.
Believe me, I tried.

But this is just fun and games.
Here's why it'll never work:
1. He's the new ER doctor in my gossipy small town.
2. He's twice my age.
3. I keep telling myself I hate him.

Even when he surprises me by showing a sweet side.

**Now that I'm having his twins,
Could Dr. Dick become Mr. Right?**

LET'S STAY IN TOUCH!

Join the Crystal Monroe newsletter for updates on new releases, sales and giveaways.

You'll get a **free romance book** when you sign up!

Click Here for a Free Book!

Or type this link in your browser:

https://dl.bookfunnel.com/j7r7vsg064

CHAPTER 1

LUKE

I wasn't in the habit of eavesdropping on hot women at the bar.

But it was hard *not* to overhear the sexy brunette as she chatted loudly with her friend.

Even harder not to sneak peeks at her.

I leaned back on my barstool and snuck a sideways glance at the woman a few seats down.

She wore a skirt that hugged her hips and thighs. A sleeveless top hinted at round, perky breasts. Long brown hair cascaded down her shoulders.

Her pouty pink mouth opened in laughter as she threw her head back.

"I don't know, Tamara." She grinned. "I don't think I'm cut out to be a tarot card reader."

She wrapped her puffy lips around the straw of her cocktail and sucked.

Shit.

I looked away before I lost my balance and fell off the stool.

"I know, I've got it!" Her friend clapped her hands. "You could be a stripper!"

She scoffed. "I'd be the worst stripper in the history of stripping. I'd trip over my high heels the first song and need a medical escort from the stage."

I brought my whiskey to my lips and focused on the burn as it went down.

It took all my concentration to pretend I hadn't just heard this sexy-as-hell woman joking about medical escorts.

I hid my smile behind my glass as she bubbled with laughter at her own joke.

She was gorgeous.

"Oh, stop. You'd fit right in with Peachwood's booming night scene." Her friend, a redhead, laughed. "You have that banging dancer bod."

I had to agree with that one. She was the whole package.

"It would be like a movie!" The brunette giggled, now going along with the idea. "By day, Hallie Jones, hardware consultant. By night? Jade Champagne, dancer of your dreams."

Hallie. I had a name.

"*Jade Champagne?* Really?"

Hallie scoffed. "I did an online stripper name generator when I was bored at work."

"So it's meant to be!"

The two women were laughing so hard I couldn't help but grin.

The idea of the petite beauty gyrating on stage stirred up tempting images in my mind. Not that I made a habit of going to strip clubs.

Still, if she were the main attraction...

"Let's be honest, Hal. If you ended up on stage, it would be for spoken-word poetry, not for stripping."

"Don't limit my creative process!" Hallie exclaimed.

My eyes were drawn to Hallie's plump lips as they pulled into a bright smile. God, I hadn't wanted a woman like this in a long time.

"All right, all right. You express yourself however you like, Miss Jade Champagne. In the meantime, I'm going to the ladies' room."

The redhead ruffled Hallie's hair and stood, leaving Hallie alone.

She took a sip of a fruity-looking girl drink. I drained the rest of my whiskey, stood, and walked over.

"Spoken-word poetry, huh?"

She jumped slightly at the sound of my voice behind her. She set her glass down and turned to me. Her doe eyes were wide as if she'd been caught doing something naughty.

If only.

"Um, my friend exaggerates. I've never actually done that. Or *anything* on stage."

"Ah. What *do* you do, then?"

The bright smile returned to her face. She rolled her eyes playfully. "I work at a hardware store. I don't really have a career yet. I just graduated from college."

Damn. She was young. She had to be about fifteen years younger.

But did it really matter in the grand scheme of things?

"Mind if I sit down?" I asked.

"Go ahead."

I took the empty seat and gestured for the bartender to bring us another round.

She glanced across the bar, locating her friend. Tamara was laughing with a guy at one of the tables.

"Looks like my friend got delayed on her way to the ladies' room."

"Looks like it."

Thank God. I'd been dying to catch Hallie alone.

She moved her hair to her far shoulder, exposing her delicate neck. "It's a small town. Everyone knows everyone."

"Yeah, I get that impression." And I couldn't wait to get to know *her*.

The bartender set the drinks in front of us, and Hallie smiled at me.

"Thanks for the drink." She stirred her cocktail with the straw.

"Sure." I eyed her. "So, you just graduated. And you haven't thought about your future? Bad girl." I gave her a naughty smile and clicked my tongue.

Hallie blinked. "What gives you the impression that I don't think about my future? The whole reason I'm here drinking is to talk about my doomed career plans."

"Why are they doomed?"

"Do you really want to know?" Gorgeous green eyes measured me up.

"Yes."

She leaned forward. Her flowery perfume flooded my senses. This woman was intoxicating.

I was more than tempted to take her back to my hotel room. I could make her forget both her real name *and* her ridiculous stripper name.

"Well, they're doomed because I don't have any."

"None?"

"I don't have a single clue what to do with my degree!"

"Well, what's your degree in?" I asked, squaring my shoulders. I liked this conversation. It put me in problem-solving mode.

"English," Hallie stated.

I sucked in a breath. "English?"

"*What?*" Her tone was defensive. As if she'd been waiting to defend this choice since she'd made it.

I shrugged my shoulders. "Nothing. Just... huh. English."

Hallie squinted at me, her eyes fiery. "Something wrong with that?"

"Yeah, actually. Obviously."

"Obviously?"

"How are you supposed to make money? If you don't know what to do with a degree, it's useless."

Hallie sighed. "Who asked you, anyway?"

I smirked. "You did. You asked if there was something wrong with your degree."

Her cheeks flushed pink. She was even prettier up close. My gaze trailed over her features for a moment. She looked away to sip her drink.

"Well, you can think whatever you like. But it doesn't give you the right to judge me."

She turned back to face me and wiped her full lips with the back of her hand. I fought back an amused smile. She was feisty.

"It shows insecurity for you to assume I'm judging you. I'd work on that."

She glared at me. I beamed and continued.

"Why would you study something you're not going to make money at?" I asked, perplexed. "Why resign yourself to becoming Jade Champagne?"

Hallie's eyes widened. She was caught off guard. "So you've been eavesdropping?"

I held my hands up. "Hey, I'm not the hot chick shouting about becoming a stripper at a bar, okay?"

Her annoyed expression changed to pure amusement. "I guess that's fair. I don't really strip, though. In case that's the only reason you decided to come over here."

I raised a brow. "Not even to shower? I've never met a hardcore never-nude before. I thought they were a myth."

She laughed, her voice feminine and lilting. "That was a

dumb joke," she added quickly. "I'm laughing because it's dumb, not funny."

She flashed a grin at me.

"You're avoiding the question," I said, rubbing my chin. It was getting stubbly. "Why'd you major in English? It was clearly a bad move. You're already questioning your life choices and shouting about stripping."

"I wasn't shouting." She pressed her hand to her chest, making her perfect cleavage bulge out of her top. "*You* were eavesdropping."

I let out a low chuckle. "You're still avoiding the question."

"I'm passionate about it, okay? Is it so hard to believe I'd choose a career I love over being miserable in a job that makes a lot of money?"

"*I'm* not miserable in my career."

"Good for you." Hallie raised her brow at me. "Are you trying to lecture me or pick me up?"

"Just offering some friendly advice to a young graduate. You could try an internship, you know. Or grad school."

"All right, all right." Hallie raised her hand. I liked the fire burning in her eyes. "Your unsolicited advice is noted. Now tell me something."

"What's that?"

"Are you going to ramble about things that are none of your business all night, or are you going to ask me to dance?"

I smirked. "We could skip to that part if you want."

"Yes, let's."

She pushed herself off her barstool on my side. My entire body sizzled from the heat of her body brushing lightly against me.

I put my hand on the small of her back to guide her to the dance floor. "I'm Luke, by the way."

"Hallie." She smiled. "But you probably already eavesdropped that part."

I couldn't help but smile back. She wasn't wrong, and we both knew it.

"Nice to meet you, Hallie."

"You, too, Luke."

We joined a few other couples on the dance floor. Hallie began to dance to the pop song they were playing. I moved to the beat, watching her hips shake as she spun around.

She looked me up and down. "You're pretty good at this. I would've expected you to be a terrible dancer."

I laughed. "Why's that?"

She shrugged. "Guys who lecture girls on career choices don't typically have good moves."

I smiled down at her. "Don't worry, Hallie. I know *all* the right moves."

She rolled her eyes and laughed as she twirled around, shaking her round hips. Her skirt was stretched tight over that perfect, heart-shaped ass.

The music changed to a slow song. She took a step closer before looking up at me with a shy smile. Then she raised her arms to rest her hands on my shoulders.

"You're strong," she said. "Do you work out or something?"

"Nah. I don't need to work out. That would be my good genes."

Hallie smirked. "Is that so?"

I nodded, trying to keep a straight face. "Yes, my family is blessed with genetics that make us all sculpted like Greek gods. In fact, my great-great-grandfather may or may not have been Zeus."

"You're ridiculous."

She swatted at my chest. When her palm made contact with the firm muscle, her eyes widened.

I rested my hands on her tiny waist and pulled her closer. "I'm just honest."

She shook her head, captivating me with another dazzling grin.

"You, my dude, have some of the weirdest pickup strategies of all time."

I pulled her a bit closer, but it wasn't enough. Not nearly.

CHAPTER 2

HALLIE

"*H*ere, have a seat," Luke said.

I didn't want to be impressed that the guy had just pulled a chair out for me. But I liked it anyway.

"Thanks. I planned on it."

I sat at the table to catch my breath. We had danced up a storm out there. It was nice to have a break.

"Are you up for another drink?"

He towered over me, his shoulders a mile across.

My heart tremored in my chest, but I played it cool. "Sure."

"Okay. I'll grab another round."

As he walked toward the bar, I took a second to collect myself.

My *God*, was this guy hot.

Like out of a steamy dream hot. He'd joked about being related to Zeus, and I was half-inclined to believe it.

Luke's build was huge, with meaty biceps and thick forearms peeking out from his rolled-up shirt sleeves. He wore his button-down shirt, jeans, and fancy watch like he was doing them a favor.

And his eyes. Good Lord, those eyes… I could get lost in that intense blue forever.

The *I'm good in bed* vibes were very strong with this one.

Not that I was considering it. I never had one-night stands.

Still, though. Luke was tempting me. Despite his arrogant lectures.

When he returned to the table, I pulled my eyes away from his tightly muscled body and focused on the glass he set down in front of me.

His sharp blue eyes weren't having it. They demanded my attention.

He grinned at me before running a hand through his dark brown hair and glancing around. "Where's your friend?"

"Oh, she's fine. I already texted her."

I nodded toward the other end of the club, where Tamara was dancing wildly with a guy of her own.

Not that Luke was *my guy*. More like a sexy but annoying amusement.

"Glad to see she's not lost without you," he jibed.

"*Hey.* She'd totally be lost without me."

He chuckled, his voice a low rumble, and I nearly shivered. Why was I so attracted to this man?

"Tell me more about yourself, Hallie." He slipped into the seat across from me. He held my gaze even more firmly than the glass of whiskey in his hand. "I'm curious."

"What, so you can keep judging me on my life choices?" I asked, keeping my tone lighthearted.

Luke smiled. "Maybe if you tell me about them, I'll understand."

I took a slow drink, then set my glass down. I was enjoying talking to this guy, despite his nosiness.

"Fine. If it's for science, I guess I could do that."

"For science," Luke vowed, lifting his glass to clink it against mine. I chuckled and followed suit. We both drank, eyeing one another over the rims of our glasses.

"Well. I went to college at New York University."

"Impressive."

"And I got my English degree there."

"Less impressive."

I rolled my eyes. The nerve of this guy. "Yes, I'm aware of your feelings on it, thank you. Now, do you want me to keep talking or not?"

"By all means."

"Why thank you, oh, all-knowing one." I took another drink and leaned back against my seat. "Anyway, I thought I could do something interesting with my degree. But when I visited the career guidance center last year, my most viable options were disappointing."

"How so?"

I sighed, noting how loose-lipped and comfortable I'd become with this guy. Hopefully, I wouldn't regret it later. For now, I was happy to keep talking. "I don't really like either of them."

"No? What are they?"

"Copywriting and..." I gave an exaggerated shudder. "Marketing."

"Marketing could make a lot of money," Luke pointed out.

"But it's *marketing*."

"But it's *money*."

"I know this might be hard for you to understand, Mr. Rolex, but sometimes it's not about the money. I want to do something creative. Something important. I don't want to be the brains behind why some guy chose to get the cedar-scented deodorant over the car-scented."

"There's car-scented deodorant?" Luke wrinkled his nose.

I rolled my eyes, though I couldn't help but laugh. "Beside the point!"

"Right. Get to the point then."

I felt a prickle of annoyance but plowed on. "Marketing is not for me, Luke. Accept it and move on."

"Okay." He sipped his whiskey, looking at me.

"And what do you do that's so great, Mr. Know-It-All?"

"I'm an ER doctor," he said.

I slumped in my seat. "Fine. That's kind of okay, I guess."

He grinned. "And I became one because it was a practical choice. It makes money. Something an English degree doesn't do."

I rolled my eyes and stuck out my tongue at him.

"How old are you? If you don't mind my asking."

I instantly regretted the tongue thing.

Plus, Luke was quite a bit older than I was, so part of me *did* mind him asking. What if it scared him off?

As annoying as he was, I was enjoying his company. In a weird way.

"I'm twenty-two."

"And you don't have your career figured out yet? Twenty-two without a clue what to do?"

I fidgeted with my napkin. "I'm sure you popped out of the womb knowing *exactly* what you wanted to do."

"That's right. They say I grabbed a scalpel right out of a doctor's hand and cut my own umbilical cord. They put me to work immediately."

"Oh my God," I said, laughing despite myself. "You're really obnoxious, you know that?"

The bright, handsome smile that parted Luke's lips had me spellbound for a moment.

Then I remembered that obnoxiousness wasn't a good thing.

"It's past time for you to figure out where your life is heading, Hallie. Your best years are wasting away right in front of you. You've got to take control of your future."

Oh, yeah. Obnoxiousness was *definitely* not a good thing.

"Are you sure you're a doctor and not some kind of wannabe life coach?"

"I failed out of the life coaching class. Plan B was medical school." Luke winked.

I scoffed and hid my smile with my glass as I took another sip. "Unfortunate. You could be *changing* lives right now instead of saving them."

He laughed, his voice deep and low.

I caught Luke's eyes and was shocked by how blue they were. I looked away again.

"You're right," I admitted. "I need to figure this out. I just want to be sure I make the right choice. It's harder than you think."

"Well, maybe if you'd chosen a more practical degree, you wouldn't be struggling so much right now." He gave another smug smile. I was about to snap at him when he interrupted. "So, why did you go from NYU to Peachwood, Georgia? I don't take this to be much of a tourist destination. Do you live here now?"

I prickled. I loved Peachwood, and he seemed to have a different opinion. But I didn't want to hear it.

"I moved back here because it's my home. And I happen to love it here. As hard as it may be for you to believe that."

"I said no such thing. You've been back here a while?"

"Just moved back in with my parents two weeks ago."

I cringed after I said it. *So much for not sounding like a kid.*

I cleared my throat. "They've been pressuring me to take over their business."

"What sort of business? Are they English majors, too?"

Luke's eyes sparkled. I ignored the comment.

I also tried to ignore the strange heat his attention made unfurl through my body.

"No. They own a hardware store."

"Ah. The store you're working at now."

"Yeah, but I'm not sure I want to take the business over. I have my own plans, you know?"

Luke raised his brow at me. "Really? Sounds to me you're blowing around like a leaf in the wind. You've got to be firmer about what you want out of life. Otherwise, life will decide for you."

"I'm not a leaf in the wind," I said with a pout.

"No? Is that why you're twenty-two and complaining to a perfect stranger about how you have no idea what to do with your future?"

I felt a spike of agitation in my chest and looked away.

Who was this guy, and why did he think he knew enough about me to make these assumptions? It was starting to piss me off.

"It's really none of your business, you know."

"True. But I'm a doctor. I like to help a charitable case."

I looked up sharply, ready to snap at him. But the sheer amusement on his face made me hesitate.

He was just teasing me. And he was thriving on my reaction at this point.

He didn't *really* think of me as a charity case.

And if he did, I was one he wanted to sleep with.

Why was the feeling so mutual? Damn good-looking men and their hold on me. Just another thing to add to the list of annoying things about this guy.

I couldn't lose my cool around him. He already thought I was just an irresponsible kid. Why give him reason to validate his opinion?

"I think it's your turn, Mr. Esteemed ER Doctor."

"My turn, Miss Jade Champagne?"

Okay, so a little bit of my irritation tended to ebb away whenever he made a stupid joke. But just because I was laughing didn't mean he wasn't an asshole. I had to remember that.

"Yes, it's your turn. We've gone through my bad life choices enough for one day."

"I don't have any bad life choices to talk about. I'm a doctor. I didn't get a degree in English, and I'd tell my parents to go to hell if they wanted me to take over some crummy business."

I shot a look at Luke, and he fixed a quick, almost apologetic smile on me. I'd have stomped away right then if he wasn't so damned kissable.

I narrowed my eyes. "Does this strategy usually work when you're trying to pick up women at bars? Eavesdropping and lecturing them about their future?"

"Is it working on you?"

I folded my arms across my chest, annoyed at the heat rising to my cheeks. "No. Of course not."

He grinned. "Too bad."

I rolled my eyes, but I was glued to my seat. Something about this guy kept me wanting more.

"It's not a crummy family business," I said evenly. "It's just not for me."

"Well, then my last piece of unsolicited advice for you is to try to figure out what is."

I hadn't expected the gentle tone Luke spoke with. I stammered when I spoke. "Yeah, sure. Whatever you say. Because it's *so* easy."

"It could be if you try out some different options."

I rolled my eyes. Enough was enough. If we didn't stop

talking about this, I'd get too irritated to find out what those lips tasted like.

"Well, since you have your life figured out, it's time you tell me more about yourself."

Luke fixed a cocky but sexy smile on me, and I seethed.

"Gladly."

CHAPTER 3

LUKE

This girl was so much fun to tease.

And honestly, it came from a good place. I couldn't let a beautiful woman full of potential waste the rest of her life.

If I could help her as I passed through this little town, then I would. She didn't have to understand that. Maybe she would one day.

Until then, I'd just have to put up with the fiery look in her eyes when I gave her advice. Which was perfectly fine by me. She was even sexier when she was mad.

"Well, you already know that I'm an ER doctor."

"Yeah? So, what are you doing in Peachwood?"

I shifted in my seat. Truth be told, I'd come to Peachwood for a job interview. The hospital here was surprisingly sophisticated for a small town.

But I didn't tell her that. I liked to keep my cards close to my chest.

"Just passing through."

"Where are you from?"

"Atlanta."

"Fancy."

I smiled. "Something like that."

"Anything else I should know about you, Doctor?"

Those dazzling green doe eyes ensnared me. For the thousandth time that night, all thoughts were driven from my mind and replaced by a growing need to have her in my bed. Now.

"Actually, yes."

Hallie arched her brow at me, stoking the fire in my abdomen. "Well?"

"You should know that there are so many things I want to do right now. And none of them involve talking."

A pink flush crept across her cheeks, and she bit back a soft sigh. I'd affected her.

My cock stiffened slightly. I wanted her, and the feeling was mutual.

I brushed my thumb over her soft cheek. Her pouty lips parted. I traced her bottom lip with my finger, her wide eyes watching me the whole time.

She leaned in, closing her eyes. I pressed my mouth against hers. She opened her lips, allowing me in.

This girl tasted sweet as candy, and I wanted more.

A tiny little whimper escaped from her throat. I kissed her deeper. I couldn't get enough of her.

Her hand moved to my knee, and she clutched the fabric of my jeans in her fist.

Fuck. Any control I'd kept on my erection was lost. My cock strained at her touch on my leg.

We broke apart. She blinked at me, her chest rising rapidly with her breath.

I took her tiny hand in mine and drew it to my lips. My eyes didn't leave hers when I spoke.

"Would you like to come and see my room at the Peachwood Inn?"

Her lips parted as she drew a breath. She nodded, all thoughts seemingly driven from her mind.

"Uh-huh," she murmured.

Her eyes were heavy and lidded as if she were in a trance. Holy *shit*, she was hot.

"Be right back."

I ran a hand through my hair, willing my cock to back off. Then I stood and went to pay both our tabs, and her friend's, too.

Hallie was texting as I approached the table. Chewing on her bottom lip, she dropped her phone in her purse and slung the bag over her shoulder. Her big green eyes looked up at me.

"All set?" I asked.

"All set."

I looped my arm around her waist and led her to the door. Outside, she leaned into me as we walked. Her soft, tight body felt good against mine.

At my car, she let out a low whistle when she saw it. I opened the door for her, and she ducked inside.

I started the engine and pulled out of the parking lot, trying not to let my eagerness show. It was hard to focus on the road with the sizzling need growing in my pants.

"This is the quietest I've seen you since we met," I teased.

"Just wondering if I should jump out of the car at the next stoplight."

She laughed. The sound made me grin from ear to ear. I moved my hand to her lower thigh and squeezed. She rested her hand on mine as I drove.

By the time we made it to the hotel, I was certain that if I didn't have her soon, I would lose my mind.

I managed to stay composed enough to walk through the lobby and swipe my key card at my room. But the second she crossed the threshold and the door closed behind us, all bets were off.

My lips pressed against hers, and God, they were so much sweeter than I remembered from fifteen minutes ago.

She slid her hands up my arms just as she had when we'd danced. I felt the shift in her timidness as her own desire began to take over.

"Do they look as good as they feel?" she murmured, her fingertips trailing up my arms. Her touch made a hot shiver surge through my spine.

"Absolutely," I teased, loosening the collar of my shirt and beginning to unbutton it.

"No." She pressed my hands aside and took the task over. "More kissing, please."

I grinned at her, happy to oblige.

I pressed into a smoldering kiss, allowing my hands to begin roaming the warm curves of her body. She gasped when I grabbed her ass and gave it a firm squeeze.

At that point, she had my shirt fully unbuttoned. She pushed it down my arms and I surrendered her rear just long enough to let my shirt fall to the floor. Then I slid my hands over the silky skin of her thighs.

"God…" she moaned.

I lifted the skirt up around her waist, needing desperately to touch her bare flesh. My palms made their way to her ass cheeks. I teased at her panties, and she shivered against me. My cock was so swollen for her it was almost painful.

"You're so sexy," I murmured into her ear.

Grasping her hips, I began to press her backward. Once we reached the bed, I pushed her gently down onto it.

She gasped, her pink mouth open and round.

I knelt between her knees and drew her leg over my shoulder, running a hand up the outside of her smooth thigh.

"I want to taste you," I said. Understatement of the

century, but I behaved enough to kiss up her thigh as my fingertips teased the lace of her panties. "Lie back and relax."

She bit her lip, then lay on her back.

"Good girl," I growled, my appetite for her growing with every second I touched her body. I didn't think twice about tearing the thin strap of her panties and pushing them to the side.

"Hey!" she exclaimed, fixing a glare on me.

I peeked up at her with a smirk. "I'll replace them. Promise."

She let out a huffy sigh, one that turned immediately into a moan as I pressed my lips against her middle for the first time. I growled as her nectar reached my lips, moving my tongue carefully as I explored.

"*Fuck*, that feels good," she whimpered. She almost sounded grumpy about it.

For some reason, it made my cock ache even more.

I pulled my tongue along her warm folds until I reached her clit. I zeroed in on the epicenter of her pleasure. Her hips jerked in response.

She let out a sharp sigh. I grinned, using one hand to unbuckle my belt and the other to caress her hip bone.

"You taste amazing," I murmured, pressing a light kiss against her clit. She shivered beneath my touch.

I couldn't hold myself back much longer. I gripped both sides of her waist and pulled her closer to my face. "Grind if you want to. Go wild."

She gasped at the sudden repositioning. I tasted her response to my words.

Still, I could sense her hesitation to let loose. But once I began my work again, easing her hips against me to start their rhythm, her reservations began to slip away.

I grunted in approval as her hips moved with the thrusting of my tongue. Her breath quickened.

I knew it wouldn't be long until I felt her undoing right against my lips.

My cock was screaming to be inside her, but it would have to wait. I was enjoying this too much.

Hallie's body writhed against the bed. I doubled my efforts to collect as much of her nectar on my tongue as I could.

She squirmed against me, swelling moans escaping from her lips. She was close now.

I buried myself against her like a man who didn't need air to breathe and took over the movement of her hips with my hands.

It took everything I had not to free my throbbing cock and thrust it inside of her to finish out her orgasm. Instead, I pressed her over the edge with the power of my tongue.

Hallie's climax curled through her body, and she closed her eyes. I watched her as she came.

She was so fucking gorgeous.

She clamped her thighs around me, gripping my hair in her fist. Her moans reached the ceiling and rang in my ears like a melody. I devoured every drop of her I could get.

Finally, the tension in her body relaxed. Her chest rose and fell as she caught her breath. I kissed just below her navel before pulling away.

I half expected her to gather her things, thank me for the orgasm, and get lost.

But she surprised me with a lopsided smile beneath tousled hair.

And then, much to the relief of my burning cock, she spoke.

"Your turn."

CHAPTER 4

HALLIE

I'd had sex before, sure. Once, I'd even had multiple orgasms during a session with my first boyfriend.

But nothing compared to the insatiable burning that Luke stirred in my body.

I couldn't get enough.

At first, I thought maybe he'd want me to go down on him, but he surprised me by immediately standing after I came. He retrieved a condom from a bag on the nightstand and tore open the package.

I gaped at the impressive size of his cock as he sheathed it in the rubber.

He didn't want a blow job. He wanted *me.*

I bit my lip as he made his way to me. He gripped my skirt in his hands, tugging it roughly down my legs and letting it fall to the floor.

His eyes raked over me as I helped him by pulling my blouse over my head. I thought for a moment that he was going to devour me with kisses, much the way he had immediately tasted my pussy, but he surprised me again.

He flipped me to my stomach and propped me up by the waist. I let out a gasp, my body flooding with heat as his cock teased my entrance.

I'd never wanted anyone like this before. It was *intense*.

Luke grunted in approval as he began to slide his rock-hard length up and down my middle. I found myself waiting impatiently, hungry for his inches. I'd never wanted someone inside me this badly before.

I shivered, heat spindling through my body as his fingertips brushed down my back. He unclasped my bra. It fell down my arms, and he reached around to fondle my breasts.

I gasped, my hips bucking against him as he took a nipple between strong fingers and began to tease it. How was he not ravishing me yet?

"Please…" I murmured.

"Please, what?"

I twisted around to see that smirk on his face. Damn him. He wanted me to beg.

"Please, Luke," I whispered. "Please fuck me."

He chuckled, then gripped my hip with one hand, his cock with the other. He pressed himself firmly inside of me.

"*Fuck*," we gasped in unison.

We might have laughed at that under normal circumstances, but I was breathless as he began to work himself inside me. He filled me up completely.

I felt every movement of his cock as he tested me, going at a pace I knew was restrained, for my sake more than his own.

But I wanted to see what he was capable of. My body pressed invitingly against him, urging him. I heard him hiss as I worked his cock, until his firm hand pressed against the small of my back, stilling me.

He used his other hand to brace himself against my hip

and began to fuck me in earnest. I didn't expect the raw power of it and nearly collapsed on the bed.

He held me firm, as if anticipating it. Wave after wave of bliss crashed through me.

How was it that I was already so close to orgasm again? It should be illegal for a man to be this good in bed.

I shuddered as he wrapped a hand around me to find my clit with his fingers. A surge of warmth gripped me.

The added pleasure made my brain swim. All thoughts were driven away with the intensity of feeling.

I was shocked by the suddenness of my next orgasm, but Luke didn't seem to be.

He worked steadily at my clit as I contracted around his cock. I arched my back and let the climax overtake me.

My arms began to wobble, and he snaked his arm around me to prop me up. As soon as I'd recovered enough, he flipped me on top of him. He lay beneath me, urging my hips against his cock insistently.

"How have you not come yet?" I panted.

He grinned at me. I'd almost forgotten how infuriatingly handsome the cocky man's face was.

"Stamina."

He thrust himself inside me so deeply that every thought in my head was driven from my mind.

I gasped, a low moan deep in my throat as need began to take over.

More.

I wanted to make him come with me. To hell with his stamina.

I began to ride his cock, nothing existing in my head but the goal of driving him to his peak.

Luke's fingers traveled my body. He gazed at me like I was a goddess, and I liked having that effect on him. It made the heat between my legs roar like an inferno, and I rode him relentlessly as I worked us both toward our climaxes.

Luke's body tensed beneath me. He was close. My breath began to quake as I felt myself surrendering along with him. Luke craned his neck against the pillow, closing his eyes.

I climaxed around his cock as he did the same inside me.

Luke grunted as his cock throbbed and released. His fingertips dug into the flesh of my waist, holding me in place as we rode out our mutual orgasms.

Slowly, his grip relaxed. His hands slid down my legs and dropped to his sides.

"Damn," he murmured.

"Damn," I agreed, sliding from my position and releasing him from my body's tight grip.

He sighed in pleasure as I lay beside him. I didn't expect that big, muscular arm to scoop around my shoulders, but it did.

I relaxed my head against him and smiled. It was surprisingly comfortable.

"I think you were right," I said.

"Well, of course I was." He paused. "About what?"

I rolled my eyes. The nerve of this guy. Still, I couldn't help but smile.

"You were right when you said this was way better than talking more."

His chest rumbled in silent laughter. "See? Maybe I know what I'm talking about. You should try taking my advice."

I groaned. "Luke, if you weren't so hot, I would have dipped out on you by now."

He fluttered his eyelashes. "You think I'm hot?" he asked in a silly voice.

I laughed, then gave his muscular body a once-over. "Uh-huh."

He really, really was. And God, the things that he'd made me feel. I'd never experienced anything like it.

The longer I looked at him, the more aware I became of the heat curling through my core. Would I ever get enough of him?

He must have known what I was thinking because he smiled.

"You're not so bad yourself, you know."

"High praise," I said, rolling my eyes. He brought his hand to my cheek, giving me no choice but to get lost in his intense blue eyes.

"I'm serious, Hallie. You're fucking gorgeous."

My heart did that obnoxious tremoring thing it liked to do with this annoying man, and I melted against him in a sizzling kiss.

It left my entire body aching for him. He seemed to sense it, because he pulled me back on top of him with gentle hands.

"Let me give you a token of my appreciation," he teased.

I gasped as I felt his body responding to me.

Then I let myself get lost in the ride.

~

I had to hand it to him. For an older guy, Luke's stamina amazed me. We had a wild night. Hell, I didn't know nights like that *existed*.

I woke up just as the sun was rising and gazed at the man tangled in the sheets beside me.

Yeah, he was still just as attractive as he had been before I'd fallen asleep. Only now, he appeared to be dreaming. Troubled dreams at that.

I almost felt bad to leave him alone like that. I almost wanted to stay in his arms.

But that was silly. It had been a fun night with a sexy man who was passing through town. And I had an amazing time.

I smiled as I sent for an Uber. Truth be told, it was kind of a relief that he would be going back to Atlanta soon. I wouldn't have been bold enough to enjoy my time with him quite the same way if I thought I'd see him in Peachwood again.

No, this was for the best. I made my escape quietly, proud of myself for going outside my comfort zone. My first one-night stand.

I ducked into the Uber and greeted the driver with a smile I couldn't restrain. I'd had a great night. It had been fun, but I had to leave the irritating doctor behind.

I took one last look at the outside of the inn. It might have been the best sex of my life, but Luke sure was a cocky bastard.

He would return to Atlanta and become a memory for me. I'd never have to deal with his insufferable lectures again.

So why did I have a lump in my throat as the car drove away?

CHAPTER 5

LUKE

I smiled as I turned to face Hallie, my body already indicating that it was ready for another round of mind-blowing sex.

I hadn't ever been with someone who was so in tune with my physical needs before. I knew she'd had the time of her life, but she might have been surprised to find that she'd impressed me as well.

When I opened my eyes, ready to ask Hallie if she had rested enough for a repeat performance of the night before, I realized that I was in the bed alone.

I stretched before rolling out of bed, not bothering to conceal my nakedness as I made my way to the bathroom. Maybe she'd be there, and I could surprise her in the shower.

I quickly realized that she wasn't there either.

My heart sank with disappointment.

Snap out of it.

One-night stands were a thing that happened. There was no reason to get down about it. I'd had an amazing night, and that was that.

CRYSTAL MONROE

Besides, it was a small town. If I really wanted to find her again, it couldn't be that hard. Not that I should look her up.

She was much too young for me. Irresponsible and immature.

What was most important to me right now was to get myself in the headspace to nail this job interview at Lakeview County Hospital.

I showered, alone, and took care of the built-up lust that my night with Hallie had left burning in my body.

When I was finished, I had about two hours until I was due for my interview. I decided to go out and grab some coffee so I would be fully prepared for the day ahead.

I hopped in my car and drove in the direction of the hospital, stopping at a modest diner along the way.

It looked cozy, like something out of a movie about small towns and romance and people trying to make ends meet. The food always looked good in those movies, so I thought I'd try my luck at it in real life since I was in the area.

A little bell jingled in greeting when I opened the door. A sign directed me to seat myself. I looked around the restaurant and found a booth in the corner, where I slid in and was promptly handed a menu.

"Thanks," I said, smiling at the waitress.

"You're new."

"Hmm?"

The waitress, a woman a bit younger than myself but with a tired expression, beamed at me. No matter how tired she might have been, she was certainly cheerful.

"You haven't been here before, have you, honey?"

I tried to hide my discomfort and remained still in my seat. I wasn't her friend, but she was treating me like I was. I didn't trust it.

"I haven't."

"You the new doctor up from Atlanta?"

DOCTOR'S SECRET TWINS

Now, my discomfort was magnified threefold. How in the hell did she know who I was?

"Not yet. I don't have my interview until after breakfast," I replied, doing everything in my power to keep the edge out of my voice.

She didn't find it weird to be talking to me as if she knew me, but it felt weird. It *was* weird, right?

I looked around for confirmation from anyone else around me, but they were all busy eating their breakfasts. Nothing out of the ordinary to them.

"Yeah! Well, you're a shoo-in for the job. Just look at ya!" She chuckled and pulled a small notepad from her apron pocket, followed by a pencil. Instead of writing anything, she twirled it in her fingers and kept talking. "My sister works in the ER up at Lakeview. She told us they were interviewing for someone to help with the workload. It would be so great for them, poor things. Run ragged up there trying to save people's lives all the time."

"Uh, yeah. I can imagine."

So, the town was a fishbowl. Everyone knew everyone else. Hell, I had a feeling that if I asked, the waitress would be able to tell me things about Hallie too. Even if only through three degrees of separation.

How could I possibly live in a place where my business would never be my own again?

My mind drifted back to my apartment in Atlanta. It had been lonely there. Insufferably so, even before my painful split with Sabrina. I sighed through the memory, forcing myself to focus on the waitress.

"Well, what can I get for you, sugar?"

"Some scrambled eggs and wheat toast, please. And a coffee. Black."

"You got it," she said, winking at me without even writing anything down on her little pad.

She walked away and I heard her shout my request to someone in the kitchen. Things in a small town sure were different than the city.

Maybe that was a good thing. It could be a nice change of pace from the way I'd been living for the past few years with my ex. Both of us had been busy all the time with our careers, and our apartment had felt more like a place to sleep than a home.

It had only gotten worse after she'd pretty much ripped my heart straight out of my chest. But now wasn't the time to delve into all of that. I needed to stay balanced for my interview.

"Here you are, honey. One black coffee, toast, and scrambled eggs. Hope you enjoy!"

"Thanks."

"Anytime! And this is on the house, for good luck with your interview."

She gave me a friendly wink and walked away before I had the chance to say anything else to her. She probably knew that I would fight the generosity with every fiber of my being. Well played.

Okay, something like *that* would never have happened to me in Atlanta. I ate my breakfast, my mind swimming with memories of my previous life, and curiosity about what it was going to become.

What would it be like to live in a small town like this?

It was daunting, but not as daunting as going back to my old home and staying at my old job. Nothing felt worse to me than that.

If Peachwood, Georgia, could give me a new start, then that was going to be exactly what I needed. I would take it.

Plus, maybe I'd run into Hallie again.

My muscles tightened at the thought of her riding me, her perfect tits bouncing, her eyes clamped shut as she came...

No. Can't go there again.

I finished my breakfast and smiled over at the waitress, who beamed back at me from where she was serving another table. I gave her a nod of appreciation before leaving. It just felt like the right thing to do.

I left her a generous tip since she obviously wasn't going to be bringing me a check. I left feeling strange about the whole thing, but it wasn't the worst feeling in the world, to be honest. It was kind of nice in a way, that they wanted to look out for me for a moment.

The kindness was driven from my mind soon after. If I didn't hurry, I wouldn't be early for my interview, and I would have to nail this.

Small town or not, I wanted that job, and I was going to get it.

I just had to keep my mind off Hallie and our night together.

CHAPTER 6

HALLIE

"You were out all night."

"Yup."

"Why?"

I sighed, catching my father's eye from behind a piece of paper he had been holding in front of his face when I came in. His accounting books for the store were sprawled all over the kitchen table, and I knew he had been hard at work with hardware drama.

"I was busy."

"Busy, huh? Doing what?" He lowered the paper he was holding onto the table and held me fast in his paternal gaze.

Busy getting nailed by a sexy doctor from Atlanta who gave me the best series of orgasms of my life.

But my father didn't have to know that.

"Is that a new tie?" I smiled. It was a running joke between us for whenever I knew I might have found myself on his bad side.

He smiled but didn't let up.

"Yeah, actually. But flattering me isn't going to prevent

my lecture and you know it. You knew you had to work today. It's a little irresponsible to be out at all hours."

"Dad. I know what I'm supposed to be doing," I said, trying not to let my annoyance come out in my voice. "I've been on my own for ages now, remember? You don't have to treat me like a kid."

"I'm not treating you like a kid, Hal. I'm treating you like my daughter."

"Okay, well, same difference," I said with a laugh. "I know you care but try to remember that I haven't been late for work once since I came home. I haven't even called out. Even when I had food poisoning from that stupid fish fry."

My mother tittered in her seat but remained quiet, knowing my father wasn't done with his interrogation.

"Good point," my father acknowledged.

I stood awkwardly, hoping I could escape to my room, but no such luck. My father took in one of his long, dramatic breaths, indicating that he was itching to go on a tangent.

Not that he was ever cruel or out of line, but I honestly wasn't in the mood. I had been on my own for the past four years. Being at home felt stifling sometimes.

"What were you doing last night? You didn't even call."

My stomach churned as memories of my night with Luke resurfaced. God, he'd been good in bed. It was the last thing I wanted to be thinking about in front of my father.

"I was spending time with Tamara, Dad. We were out late, and I thought it would be safer to crash there than drive home tired."

I hated lying, but it seemed like a better option than telling my father the truth. He was definitely not prepared for the fact that I was a sexually active young woman. It would taint my image in his eyes forever.

"Ah. Tamara. How is she doing?"

"Well, thank you. She sends her love."

My father's face softened. "Is she still working at the hospital?"

"Yep, still doing the ultrasound tech thing." Unlike me, Tamara had picked a practical educational path. She loved her job and made decent money.

He nodded, a slight smile on his lips. "Sit and talk with me for a minute."

I hesitated, wishing I'd showered before I left the hotel, but sat reluctantly at the table across from my father.

"I'm glad you got to get out of town and spread your wings for a bit, but we all know how far that degree of yours is going to get you. It's not worth two cents."

I prickled. Why did everyone shit on my dreams lately?

"You know we have a family business. It's all you need, honey. You'll be taken care of with it."

"Well... I'm not taking anything over yet, Dad. I haven't even decided if that's what I want to do."

"Hallie, you need to have a stable and reliable source of income. It's just the way the world works. It's going to be a great opportunity for you."

"Yeah…"

"Why don't you come in to work early with me today? I can show you some of the ropes. It would help you have an idea of what it's all about."

"I want to use my degree, Dad. I'll find work with that."

"Hallie, we want you to thrive. An English degree from NYU isn't really how you're going to do it. I'm not sure why you wasted your time and all that tuition money, but I'm sure you learned a lot of nice things. Just let me help you."

I sighed. "I was actually thinking about furthering my education. I might be going back to graduate school. In Atlanta."

I didn't know where the words came from, but they could only have come from Luke. Everything he'd been saying and trying to encourage me to do. Maybe it would be enough to get my parents off my back about all of this.

"Graduate school, huh? That would be a lot of work. And a lot more money."

I could tell by my father's voice that he wasn't particularly thrilled about it.

It seemed like nothing I did would matter to people unless it was what they wanted me to do. Or unless I was making a lot of money.

"I could focus on marketing or something like my counselor at NYU said. Make money following the career path I carved out for myself. I'm sorry, but I don't want to spend the rest of my life managing a hardware store. I want to do something that interests me a little more."

Did marketing actually interest me? Hell no. But did my parents need to know that? Also hell no.

What felt important right now was to stick to my guns. I had chosen this path for a reason, and I just wanted people to respect it.

My father simply nodded and picked up his accounting papers again. I waited for a moment before I dismissed myself and walked upstairs to my childhood room.

I ran my hands along the row of stuffed animals sitting at the entrance of the room. There was nothing about this room that reflected who I was now or who I wanted to become.

I felt like a trapped kid.

The way Luke had looked at me resurfaced in my mind and I felt my cheeks growing warm.

He hadn't made me feel like a kid, even though he hadn't exactly agreed with my path either. At least he'd tried to encourage me to follow it in a smarter way, unlike my family. They just dismissed it altogether.

Well, that didn't matter. I went to my desk and turned on

my computer. I still had a few hours before I had to get ready for work.

That was enough time to write a chapter of the romance novel I'd started working on.

Now that I'd had the most mind-blowing sex of my life, I was feeling pretty inspired.

No one knew I was writing it except Tamara.

I'd kept my writing hobby a secret ever since a college professor had torn apart a short story I'd written. He was so brutal that I'd cried over it for three days.

But he didn't have to know about my novel. No one did.

I typed furiously, channeling all the excitement I'd felt with Luke into the page.

When my alarm went off, I saved the file and headed to the shower. It was time to return to *the real world* once more.

CHAPTER 7

LUKE

"I'm so glad to welcome you to Peachwood!" the brightly smiling blonde realtor said to me. She offered me a hand. "Penny Wallace Ledger, at your service!"

I chuckled and took her hand, noting the impressive wedding band on her finger. Her smile widened and she looked like she wanted to tell me all about it. Instead, she waited for me to introduce myself.

"Luke Beckett," I said, releasing her hand. "And thank you. It's quite a little place."

"That it is," Penny said. She chuckled, her green eyes twinkling. "I was so excited to hear that you were going to be working with Bruce! He's such a good guy; I just *know* you guys will hit it off and it will be a great fit!"

Well, it couldn't be any worse than my last job.

My ex, Sabrina, had managed to destroy every semblance of stability I'd tried to build. I was planning to propose. But when she cheated on me with a guy I thought was a friend from work, all bets were off.

There was no way I could keep working with him after that.

CRYSTAL MONROE

I'd been looking around for jobs and happened to land an interview at Lakeview Hospital in Peachwood. I could only hope it would be the new beginning that I needed.

Penny was right, Bruce Anglin, the hospital administrator, seemed like a genuinely good guy. I wouldn't have to worry about him snatching my partner right out from under my nose.

"I'm looking forward to a fresh start," I said to Penny, realizing that I'd gotten carried away in my thoughts.

"Peachwood is the *best* place for new starts! Take it from me." She gave me a quick wink. I had a feeling I should probably trust her authority on that one.

"Well... it's a small world, isn't it? You knowing Bruce and him knowing that I'd need a place to stay."

"I'd say so! And between you and me, he doesn't usually hire people on the spot like that. There must be something special about you. He called me right up after your interview!"

I scoffed, though the idea that I'd made an impression on the man was nice. It was good to be respected, and if I could manage to maintain that respect in this new place, maybe the fishbowl aspect wouldn't be entirely awful.

"Let me show you around."

I glanced around the house. I'd been impressed with it. It had a big yard, solid architecture, and it just looked comfortable. A far cry from my sterile little place in Atlanta. And much more affordable for so much more space.

"Lead the way."

Penny excitedly did just that. I could see myself living there. I'd have space for an office, and it was out of the way and in a peaceful neighborhood. It was kind of perfect, actually.

"Three bedrooms might seem like a lot," Penny said in conclusion, "but you never know where life might take you!

A handsome guy like you might even end up settling down and wanting a family someday."

The idea of having a family here, in this town, gave me a pause. And, for some reason, made Hallie flash in my mind.

God, no. No, no, no.

"Maybe," I said stiffly, trying to shoo the obnoxious young woman out of my thoughts entirely.

Hallie had no business being there, especially not with two kids in *my* house. No way.

Still, there was just something about her that kept my blood running hot. It was like a poison, really. I wished she would just leave my mind sometimes so I could focus.

"You came at just the right time," Penny said. "The homeowners have recently lowered the price. They're desperate to get it off the market and find someone who will close on it."

I nodded thoughtfully. I had already noticed how reasonable the price was.

It was a steal, actually, and if things didn't end up working out for me here, this would be a nice little investment. I'd be able to turn a profit and get the hell out of there at the same time.

"Let me just show you the garage and we should be all set!"

I nodded, and Penny led me to the garage. She explained all its perks and then smiled at me as I took it all in. I took a moment to think before meeting her eyes.

"I've got to be honest with you, Penny... I never saw myself living in a small town before."

Her smile faltered almost imperceptibly. She looked like she was trying to figure out the right thing to say, but I interrupted her with a reassuring smile.

"I'll take it. Is cash okay?"

Her eyes widened, and I chuckled to myself. It looked as if I had just given her a tremendous gift. She beamed at me.

"Cash is perfect. I can send the offer right to the owners of the place. But I doubt that you'll have to wait long for them to accept it. I might as well welcome you to the neighborhood right now!"

"Thank you."

The house itself seemed like it was fated. The job, and a place to live, had practically fallen right into my lap. I shouldn't look a gift horse in the mouth, right? I should be happy.

"Don't worry, you'll start to feel at home here in no time. I moved here from out of town myself. Of course, it was a bit of an adjustment for me, too. But this place has a way of working its way into your heart, and quickly. There's nothing quite like the people in Peachwood."

I had already figured that out for myself.

All day long I'd been fighting thoughts of Hallie and the ways she had made my body sing.

I'd be lying if I said I didn't want to see her again. Maybe if I set up camp in this town, I could relive the night we'd had before.

Not that I was only moving here to be with her. Obviously, that was just a bonus.

"I trust that everyone would be very welcoming to me," I said. "Everyone has seemed nothing but… inviting… so far."

"That's Peachwood for you!" Penny beamed. She really seemed to love it here. "We all look out for one another. It'll be a great experience if you let it."

I shifted my weight, once again finding myself feeling uncomfortable with the fishbowl-town lifestyle.

She laughed, shaking her head. "This kind of reminds me of when my husband moved to town. He's a doctor, too."

"Oh, yeah? What's his name?"

"Max Ledger, cardiologist. I'm sure you'll meet him." She

fixed me with a knowing smile. "He's grown to love this town, too."

"Well, I'll look forward to moving in here as soon as possible."

"Awesome! I'll be in touch with the rest of the details. It was a pleasure to meet you, Dr. Beckett. And welcome to Peachwood!"

I shook her hand with a smile and Penny left. I lingered for a moment before making my way back to my car.

Yes... Welcome to Peachwood.

CHAPTER 8

LUKE

A week later, I watched my moving truck being driven away. All of my belongings had finally been moved into the house on Peach Tree Lane that Penny had led me to. And by finally, I meant that I'd managed to get it all here in record time.

It was kind of amazing how getting the hell away from my bad memories had motivated me to get my affairs in order. I had nothing left to go back to in Atlanta at this point.

From now on, it was going to be all about moving forward.

This move had been the easiest of my life. The neighborhood was truly beautiful in its own little way. I'd already begun making myself at home in the perfect house. It really felt as if some sort of fate had intervened and brought me here after landing that job with Lakeview.

I was taking my time in figuring out exactly how I wanted to set up my space here. There were many details that I hadn't quite worked out yet. It felt strange after so long of being with Sabrina to be making executive decisions about where things were placed without worrying she would be nagging at me about it later.

Well, I wouldn't ever have to worry about that again. I had made the mistake of giving my all in a relationship once. It wasn't going to be happening again.

I didn't need it. I was a lone wolf now.

This home was mine and mine alone. It was my palace and I was having a good time settling into it.

But the curtains had to go. Whoever had sold the place thought that peach-themed everything was the ticket. I preferred something a little more neutral.

As I removed the curtain rods, I studied the neighbors' homes a little more closely.

Each had expansive, gently sloping lawns that were well-manicured. They looked beautiful.

I'd only lived in condos before. Now I would have to look into all the details of lawn maintenance. It would be strange, but I could do it. I'd done a little yard work before. Still, it would be hard to compete with these guys.

Besides, it wasn't like I planned on being in this house forever. I was only along for the ride at the moment.

This house was a stepping stone. I'd buy a larger house someday. And when I did, I would rent this little place out to a couple who wanted to have a good place to raise a family but who couldn't quite afford to keep up with the Joneses.

I chuckled to myself at the irony. When she'd given me the keys to move in, Penny had mentioned that the neighbors to my right were the Joneses. They seemed to be doing well with their two huge SUVs parked out front.

Not that I was bitter at the Joneses. I hadn't even met them yet. They were likely the same level of charming and welcoming as everyone else in the little town seemed to be. And I was sure I would find out sooner rather than later.

This wasn't like Atlanta, where I could mind my own

business for months without even noticing that a neighbor in my complex had moved away. No, everyone here saw everything you did. They would make themselves known soon enough.

There were plenty of other things I could do here, too. Like, for example, trying to run into the bombshell that had blown my mind in the bedroom the week before.

I was surprised and, honestly, a little bit disappointed that I hadn't run into her again yet. But that could change.

I remembered the bar where I'd picked her up and figured that there weren't that many different places she might be hiding out on a Friday night. If I tried my luck there a few times a week, I was bound to see her again. And if she didn't show up, I was sure the bartender would know her.

It was a small enough town after all. I wasn't above asking to get what I wanted.

My body was aching for her. Maybe she would be down for another romp.

It would be shocking if she wasn't, honestly. I could tell she had enjoyed herself just as much as I had.

She was young and kind of goofy, but no one said we had to get engaged. The sex had clearly been amazing.

Yes, I was going to find her again. I wouldn't be able to get her out of my head until I did. Until I tasted her again.

In the meantime, I had unpacking to do.

~

"Dr. Beckett! Welcome!"

I smiled and reached a hand out to greet the brown-haired doctor.

"Dr. Oliver Brian. I'll be working with you in the ER!"

"Nice to meet you, Dr. Brian. I take it you already know exactly who I am."

"Takes the fun out of introductions when you move to Peachwood," the man standing beside Dr. Brian said with an impish laugh. He jutted a hand out to me. "I'm Sam. Sam Huggins. I'm a nurse here. It's a pleasure to meet you."

"The pleasure is mine," I said, taking Sam's hand and giving it a firm shake.

"Speaking of pleasure," Sam said, lowering his voice conspiratorially and nodding his head in the direction of the nurses' station. "Little Miss Tight-Ass over there really does have a tight ass. If you know what I mean. Found that out last night."

Dr. Brian let out a laugh. "What? No way. I've been trying with her for *weeks.*"

"You weren't trying with strong enough booze then," Sam said with a cackle.

"Dude."

I stood between the men awkwardly. They were shockingly unprofessional, and it got on my nerves.

But the last thing I wanted to do the first half hour of my new job was to appear like the stick in the mud who wouldn't be okay with some lighthearted workplace banter.

Still, it was disgusting. I quickly changed the subject. "So where do we scrub in?"

"I'll show you, Beckett. Come on."

Dr. Brian had very quickly lost the formality of my title, which again, made me bristle. "Dr. Beckett. If you want to be informal, you can call me Luke."

"Oh. Right. My bad, man. Follow me."

I nodded and followed Oliver throughout the winding corridors of Lakeview County Hospital.

It was an impressive hospital for a place like Peachwood. I made note of all the features I liked about it and automatically did some compare and contrast about my own facility back in Atlanta.

CRYSTAL MONROE

It was very clean, and although it was busy, it wasn't hectic. I could tell that most of the people here took great pride in their work. Even the cleaning staff. Lakeview attracted some really prestigious doctors from Atlanta, and other areas nearby as well, me being among them.

I could see the appeal, really. The facility was a tight ship, and the administration seemed to really have the right values in mind.

And many of the doctors I'd worked with in Atlanta had wanted to get out of the city. To start fresh in a place with less of a rat race. Our jobs were already stressful enough.

Somewhere with a slower pace of life. Exactly like Peachwood.

"All right, Beckett. I mean. Luke. Here we are! You should have a locker over here too if you need it. Nobody ever messes with anyone else's stuff so there's nothing to worry about here. Unless Huggins gets himself into the women's locker room. They might have something to worry about then."

I narrowed my eyes, but Dr. Brian had already turned his back to me. "Anyway, I'll catch up with you later, Luke. I'm sure we'll be working together plenty."

"Looking forward to it," I said, although to be honest I wasn't entirely sure if that was the truth.

I could only take so much immature banter. And while I enjoyed good sex as much as the next guy, there was a time and a place for those discussions. It showed a blatant lack of respect, not just for the women they were talking about, but to the patients, staff members, and to me, really. It was unprofessional to greet me with that kind of behavior.

Maybe it bothered me more because of everything that had happened with Sabrina.

The guy she'd cheated on me with, Aaron, had been a good friend. But he'd had that immature streak in him. If I'd have known that even a man's girlfriend was fair game to him, I probably would have dropped him a lot sooner.

He even knew that I had been planning to propose. I couldn't stand the way those kinds of guys thought.

For some reason I thought again of Hallie. Would I ever dare tell someone how tight her ass was? No matter how many times I'd gotten hard over it? No.

It wasn't anyone's business.

"Dr. Beckett, welcome." I was broken out of my thoughts by a new face, friendly, but thoughtful. He was taller than the other two men. He took my hand with a shake I could respect and then looked over my shoulder at where Dr. Brian was leaving the room. "I hope you're finding everything that you need. Feel free to come to me if you have any questions."

"Thank you."

"Dr. Ryder Finley," the man said, giving me a quick smile. "I'm in neurology."

He was well kept, with dark brown hair and sharp eyes. It seemed like he would be able to size up just about any situation at a glance.

"A pleasure to meet you, Dr. Finley."

I almost bit back the words, considering pleasure had been a topic that had caused the other doctor and nurse to get rowdy. Dr. Finley seemed to sense my thoughts.

"I see you've met Dr. Brian and Sam."

"I have."

"Dr. Brian does solid work, but I'd recommend steering clear of those two. They're utter clowns."

I blinked, not certain I had heard Dr. Finley correctly. His eyes betrayed a sparkle of humor, but I could tell by the rest of his demeanor that he was serious. I'd already sensed as much from the two but could tolerate some good-natured ribbing here and there.

"I'll keep that in mind, Doctor," I said with a smile.

He smiled back. "Welcome to the team."

I nodded as Dr. Finley took his leave. It was always an adventure to navigate the social landscape of a new job. This was going to be fun.

Not as much as having another all-nighter with Hallie. But then, nothing could compare to that.

CHAPTER 9

HALLIE

"I have a job for you, Hallie."

The house smelled amazing. My mother had been baking. I could already guess what that job was going to be.

"Welcoming committee?" I asked.

Secretly, I couldn't stand being told what to do by my parents, but I was trying to stay positive. They were already on me about my career choices. Rocking the boat this early in the morning didn't seem like a wise move.

"Welcoming committee," she confirmed, handing me a plate of cookies. "We have a new neighbor and I want to make sure he feels comfortable in the neighborhood."

"Who wouldn't feel welcome with a plate of your famous chocolate chip cookies?" I asked, kissing my mom on the cheek. I looked enviously at the plate in my hands. "Were there any leftovers?"

"Afraid not."

"Oh."

"Don't pout, dear. I've got another batch in the oven for us."

I beamed. "Awesome!"

"His name is Mr. Beckett. I want you to invite him to help us work on the float. Peach Tree Lane will shine at the Independence Day Parade this year with an extra pair of hands."

"The parade will be fun," I said. "It's been too long since I got to spend it with you guys."

"I know, and the street parties haven't been the same without you. I have the picnic all planned out already."

"Do you think this Mr. Beckett will even be interested?" I asked.

My mom didn't always realize that other people weren't quite as enthusiastic about the same things she was. I didn't want the poor guy to feel pressured right away into doing something he wasn't comfortable with.

But that was apparently the way things were going to go. And I would be doing the pressuring. Of course.

"We won't know until we ask. Hurry along, dear. I'm hoping to get these to him before he's out and about for the day. You know they're best when they're warm."

"Yes, ma'am," I said with a laugh. "On my way."

I'd been vaguely aware of the moving van that had been parked next door earlier in the week but hadn't caught a glimpse of the mysterious new neighbor yet. I'd been consumed with writing my novel.

I'd had a ton of inspiration since my tryst with Luke. And I'd be lying if I said I hadn't been missing his touch.

He was heavy on my mind as I made my way out the door. I was glad I was wearing my cutoff jean shorts and a tank top. It was stiflingly hot outside. The first truly hot day of summer so far.

Maybe Mr. Beckett wouldn't even be home. That would be nice. Then I could just leave and not have to worry about making awkward small talk with a stranger, then asking him to do my mother's bidding for the parade. He'd find a plate of cookies on the porch and that would be that.

As I approached the house, I saw that the garage door was open, and a car was parked inside. I couldn't quite make out what he drove, but that didn't matter very much. What mattered was that I now had to prepare a script to speak with the new neighbor. Fun, fun.

Before I had even managed to prepare the second line of my script, the new neighbor's door opened.

I felt a spike of panic and gripped the cookies in my hand tightly so they wouldn't tumble to the ground.

Luke. It's Luke.

It took him a moment before he noticed me, but when he did, he beamed and gave me a wave. I was still clutching the cookies, which I was glad for. It meant I could stand there being dumbfounded without feeling obligated to return the wave.

This couldn't be right. Luke lived in Atlanta. He couldn't be here, living in Peachwood. And he *definitely* couldn't be my new neighbor. It was impossible.

But no, it wasn't impossible, because there he was, walking toward me with an irritatingly sexy grin on his face. It was definitely him, and this was really happening. The arrogant man I'd had a one-night stand with was my new neighbor. Worse, he was living next to my *parents.*

This was bad. Very bad.

I clutched the plate closer to my body and tried not to let the emotion show on my face. Instead, I mustered a smile.

"Hi, Mr.—er, *Dr.* Beckett," I said, reciting the first line of my script. "Welcome to the neighborhood."

CHAPTER 10

LUKE

There was no way.

Hallie looked like a deer in headlights as I made my way off my porch and headed toward her. She was holding something close to herself like a shield. I couldn't help but grin.

"Thanks," I said in response to her welcome. "You look nice."

Nice was an understatement.

Her body was radiating in the tight tank top and formfitting shorts. It made me feel like a dog for trying to calculate exactly how long it would take me to get her out of those clothes.

It took all I had not to get hard right then and there. God knew she had been on my mind enough that just hearing her voice would have been enough to do it.

But to show up looking like *this*? It was sinful.

"So... you're our new neighbor?" she asked, taking a timid step forward. The shield she held left the closeness of her body as she relaxed a little bit. "My mom wanted you to have these. As a welcome thing. Hospitality or whatever."

"Or whatever," I teased, grinning at Hallie, trying not to notice the way my body buzzed with anticipation.

Every inch of me wanted to take her right then and there. I'd thought of her so often that I could hardly contain myself.

"I thought you lived in Atlanta," she blurted. "I didn't think…"

"Well, plans change," I said, my mind searching for any possible way to hide from the awkwardness of my body's reaction to seeing her again. "Which is allowed if you know what you're doing in life. What about you? Are you still lost and aimless?"

She jutted her chin out at me like a petulant little kid, which I found adorable. I had to start running basketball statistics in my head to keep myself from producing a rather prominent erection. That was the last thing we needed right now.

She opened and closed her mouth, unable to reply to my remark. Maybe she was just as stunned to see me as I was to see her.

Either way, I couldn't just leave her hanging like this. I looked at the plate of cookies she clutched.

"I should put these inside. Why don't you come in? You know… so you can see my interior decorating skills."

I winked at her, which brought a deep flush of red across her already blushing face. She screwed up her face in a look of adorable annoyance.

"You need help."

"Are you offering?"

I knew I was being a bit of a pig. But God, I couldn't wait to touch her again. I could already see the way she was looking at me, like a dehydrated dog thirsty for some water.

She shoved the cookies at me, and I reached for them. I stiffened when I felt the warmth of her fingertips against mine as I took the plate. I was as amused as I was disappointed when she began storming off.

My eyes wandered down her body, lingering on the perfect shape of her ass in those cutoff shorts. I would have to remember to thank whoever had invented those. They had never looked so good before.

I was about to head inside, but to my surprise, Hallie turned on her heel. She fixed a glare on me and crossed her arms over her chest.

"I'm supposed to ask you if you want to work on the float for the Fourth of July Parade. It's a Peach Tree Lane thing. Since you live here, you know. It's a thing we do."

I quirked a brow at her, trying my hardest not to let out the bubble of laughter that was forming in my chest. "Sure."

"*Perfect*," she spat. Clearly, it was the absolute opposite of perfect.

When she had finally found her way inside her house, I let the laughter out.

That had gone well.

And nothing had delighted me more since moving to Peachwood than knowing Hallie was my new neighbor.

~

About an hour later, I was putting books away on my shelf when I heard a knock at the door. I frowned, confused.

I couldn't stomach any more cookies or welcoming committees unless they were Hallie and they rode my cock this time.

I sighed before I opened the door, then blinked in surprise.

"Hallie?"

She looked sheepish but offered me a quick smile. "Hi."

"Hi."

She stood on the porch awkwardly before speaking again. "Do you need help unpacking your things? I know that moving is a pain."

I repressed a grin, then made a big show of thinking about her offer. "I suppose a little help couldn't hurt. Why don't you come inside?"

"Um... all right."

"Good girl," I said with a soft laugh.

I pulled the door all the way open and held it for her, allowing her to step inside in front of me. By some miracle, she was still wearing the little number from earlier. I couldn't even stop my eyes from wandering down for a close-up of her ass.

God, it looked good in those shorts. And her legs... they went on for miles. All I could think about was spreading them.

"Why the change of heart?" I asked, trying to distract myself.

But she had entered my lair. Surely, she knew exactly what might happen here. What it might make me feel...

"I kind of just wanted to hide out for a while. My parents are giving me a hard time about my career options."

"You mean your lack of career options," I corrected.

She scoffed. "Could you not? I'm trying to get away from that stuff."

"All right," I said. "Well then, welcome to my humble abode. It's not much yet, but it's a work in progress."

"I've always liked this house," Hallie said, walking into the empty dining room and running her hand along the wooden panels of the wall. "It's really quite beautiful."

"It does have a particular charm to it. Otherwise, I might not have bought it."

Hallie nodded. "Did you get a job at Lakeview Hospital?"

"Yes. Meet Peachwood's newest ER doctor."

"It's about time they hired someone new. I hear they have their hands full."

"Yeah." My eyes flicked over at her ripe tits stretching the fabric of that tank top. I wouldn't mind getting my hands full myself.

"So, what do you need the most help with right now?"

"I've got to rearrange my bedroom furniture," I said. "I already assembled it, but moving it alone without scraping the hardwood floors is a challenge."

"I can help with that," she said with a neutral expression. She didn't blink at the invitation to my bedroom.

I nodded and led the way to my room. Once there, she surveyed the furniture with a thoughtful eye. She frowned.

"You have it all wrong. You want the bed on this wall, or else the sun will be in your eyes every morning."

I chuckled. "I take it you know that from experience."

"You take it right."

"Well, unlike *someone*, I know how to take good advice. Let's do it your way."

She scoffed, but a prideful expression lit her face underneath it.

"I think that sounds like a great idea."

"You would," I teased.

She grinned and stuck her tongue out at me. My eyes lingered on it a little longer than I intended, and she turned away. I could tell that the attention wasn't lost on her.

That delicious blush crept across her beautiful face. I felt my cock tightening against my leg as I stared at her. The basketball shorts I wore were probably a bad idea today.

If only I had known.

Then again, maybe they weren't such a bad idea after all. The next time Hallie looked at me, she saw. Then she looked me in the eye with such smoldering intensity that the only option was to fuck her.

I couldn't help myself. She moved toward me, and I grabbed her, pressing my mouth to hers.

She let out a soft moan against my lips. I wrapped my arms around her, pulling her close against my body. My rock-hard cock pressed against her soft little belly.

I'd never wanted anyone this way before. And as skimpy as her little outfit was, there were far too many clothes. I had to do something about it.

My hands worked faster than my brain as I began tearing her clothes away. First, the tank top, then the sinful little shorts. I didn't stop until all I had standing before me was her naked, quivering body.

I pressed her down onto my bed. She whimpered with need, her body tense as she lay on the sheets. I kissed down to her navel far more delicately than my frenzied state demanded.

She writhed as I finally got a taste of her. I had spent such a long time craving her delicious flavor. I was transported as my lust grew into something I could barely contain.

Apparently, the feeling was mutual, because Hallie began to bury her hands in my hair as she moaned loudly. Her sensual sounds brought goosebumps to my arms.

Her hips bucked up against me and I sank my tongue inside her. She cried out in pleasure. I reached up to massage her hips as my tongue worked itself in and out against her pooling honey.

It didn't take long before I felt Hallie's body begin to quake beneath my hands. She arched her back with a deep moan. I sped up my efforts and growled in satisfaction as she climaxed.

At that point, my cock was burning. All I wanted was to be inside of her. I caught Hallie's eye, curious.

"I want you inside me," she said. "Now."
I grinned.
"Happy to oblige."

CHAPTER 11

HALLIE

I had been waiting for him for so much longer than I was willing to admit.

The night we shared hadn't left my mind since it happened. I'd relived it constantly, even including specifics in my novel.

Now, he was climbing on top of me. I watched in anticipation as he gave my body a once-over. His intense blue eyes were hypnotizing.

And then he stopped and caught me in his gaze.

"Do you have a condom?" he asked. "I haven't had a chance to pick any up. I was so busy moving things that I didn't even think about it."

"Condom? No. Shit."

He pulled away, but I grabbed him impulsively and pulled him back. "No. It's okay. I trust you not to do anything stupid."

"I do have experience in certain techniques." He looked at me. "I can pull out."

"Then please don't stop."

He smiled, cocky but sexy, and freed his swollen cock from its confines.

"If you insist. Time to christen this place," he said with a teasing grin.

Suddenly, Luke flipped me onto my stomach and propped me up on my knees. I braced for him with my heart pounding. Anticipation welled inside me as I waited.

I gasped when I felt him slide against me, skin to skin. The sensation of him rubbing against my middle electrified me.

It took all I had not to beg him to enter me immediately. I wanted to savor the moment. It was my first time having sex without a condom, and it felt amazing.

Most of all, I was thrilled to experience the way he made me feel again. I thought it had been a one-time thing. Now that it was happening again, it was more than I'd hoped for.

I hadn't even realized how much I'd been longing for his touch.

As if to prove it, I thrust my hips so that his member was unexpectedly half-submerged in my heat. Tendrils of pleasure crept through my abdomen.

That was it. No more holding back.

I gasped. My motion had motivated him, and he pressed himself fully inside me. I felt every inch of him, and it was so much better than I remembered. Especially with no barriers between us.

He entered with a little more force than I would have expected. It shocked my body as pleasure traveled all over, right down to my fingertips. To my complete delight, he began to thrust inside me.

I let out a strangled cry of ecstasy and gripped his back. I pulled him closer into my body as his hips began their steady rhythm. The pleasure was almost too much to bear.

I could feel the tingling of electricity on my skin as my body was given permission to let go.

"How does this feel even better than the first time?" My words came out in a raspy, gasping sound. I bowed my head against the bed as he thrust inside me.

Luke was either unwilling or unable to answer. His response to me only made me want him more. My guttural groan was muffled by his bedsheets as pleasure consumed me.

Suddenly, I was weightless. Luke gripped me by the hips and moved me on top of him. I ran my fingers down his six-pack abs as I settled into the new position.

I was perfectly okay with it. I hadn't been able to get the image of riding his cock out of my head. Now I was doing it.

Thankfully.

I ached for more as his hands gripped my waist. He moved me against him, and I let out a soft gasp. Delicious friction was snaking through my core, driving every thought from my mind but Luke's cock.

I moaned as he entered me once more. My body trembled as the heat of my pleasure consumed me. I began to move my hips, and he growled.

He gripped my hips again and urged me to grind faster against him. I nearly lost my mind as my body was rocked with bliss. His sexy, chiseled face fixed on me, focused on our bodies working together in unison.

God, he was handsome. It was almost unfair, honestly. But I wasn't complaining.

Especially when he flipped me again. His strength was thrilling as he pressed me onto my back and began to thrust in earnest.

"Fuck," I breathed, unable to prevent myself from speaking. I was overwhelmed as hot pleasure pulsed inside me. I was dangerously close to coming.

He seemed to be able to sense it because he began to work in overtime. His powerful, virile body seemed almost superhuman. I cried out as I felt the first contraction of an orgasm begin to tighten around Luke's cock.

Luke's expression twisted. I knew he was close, too. But he had stamina, and he wanted to see me through first. My fingers gripped the sheets as a searing climax tore through me.

He hissed in pleasure as I began to ride out my orgasm. He managed to hold fast throughout it, then pulled out.

I moaned as I watched his cock shoot thick streams of warm, thick cum all over my stomach and breasts.

Fuck, it was hot being covered in his release.

He squeezed the last few drops out, panting. Then he stood there a moment, looking at me.

Why was I so attracted to this man? It was almost shameful.

"Wait here a second," he said, moving away from the bed. He disappeared from the room for a few moments.

When he returned, he had a towel. He sat beside me and carefully cleaned me up.

"I guess you do have experience with certain techniques," I joked quietly.

He offered me one of his trademark cocky grins.

Suddenly, I felt disgusted with myself. I couldn't let myself be fooled. He wasn't a sweet man.

In fact, he was a bona fide asshole. I'd made a huge mistake in coming to his house. Especially now that he was my neighbor.

Oh, God. He's actually my neighbor.

I sat up quickly once he was finished cleaning himself off my stomach. His brow furrowed as I scrambled to find my clothes. They were strewn all over his floor.

"What's the rush?" Luke asked, sweeping a long arm down

from the side of the bed to pick up his shorts. He pulled them on and stood to face me. I hated that he still looked so good.

"This can't happen again," I muttered, already heading for his bedroom door. "I just had to get that out of my system if you're going to be living right next door."

I made a beeline for the door. I could hear Luke chuckling behind me like he thought I was being a petulant little kid.

Whatever. Let him think what he wanted. I had things to do.

I made my way back home and immediately went up to shower. I had to scrub whatever remnants were left of Luke's semen from my body. There was no way I'd go to work with any trace of that cocky jerk's fluids on me.

Once I was finished, I checked the time and felt a spike of panic. My dad would be waiting for me at the hardware store. The last thing I needed was another lecture.

Fortunately, I made it to work on time. Whatever was in store for me wouldn't involve my tardiness. That was a plus.

"Hallie, come here."

I looked around the hardware store, my chest constricting. "Okay, Dad."

I found him behind the counter, adjusting rows of screws on the wall. "I need you to do inventory today."

I shriveled. He knew I hated doing inventory. It felt like a punishment for trying to assert myself before I decided to make a break for it and visit Luke.

"All right, Dad."

He gestured to his left, not even bothering to look at me as he spoke. "I need you to work on the power tools. Make sure you hustle. There are other things that need to be done, too."

"Okay."

I bit my tongue, knowing that if it was a punishment, calling it out wouldn't do any good. Neither would trying to tell him I didn't want to do it. I was at a standstill and just had to do my job.

As I made my way to the power tools, the narrow aisles seemed almost as if they were closing in on me. I took a deep breath to ward away the claustrophobic feeling. The store was as narrow as my parents' perspective.

I didn't want to do this for the rest of my life.

There was no way I'd be able to. I began with my task, wondering what Luke must have thought when I'd run away earlier.

He had been laughing at me, so maybe he had expected it.

Maybe he didn't think I meant what I said about getting it out of my system.

The idea made me furious. But... what if I *didn't* mean it? I could already feel an ache for him. All just from thinking about him. It seemed so unfair.

Of all the people in the world for my stupid body to fixate on, why did it have to be this arrogant bastard?

And why was he now my next-door neighbor?

I sighed and shook my head, trying to focus on the inventory.

I'd just have to ignore the burning desire I felt for that cocky jerk.

CHAPTER 12

LUKE

The last time, huh?

I didn't like the sound of that. In fact, I wanted to make sure that it would most definitely *not* be the last time.

And I knew exactly how to do it. All I had to do was wait for my next day off from work.

I was getting my mail when a voice called out to me.

"Dr. Beckett! So lovely to see you! I take it my daughter delivered my message to you?"

I offered my most charming smile to the woman who approached me. I knew it was Hallie's mom right away. My mind registered the words. Then wandered to the way Hallie had looked spread naked on my bed.

"Oh, she delivered," I said with a private smirk.

"Wonderful! I wasn't sure I would be able to rely on her for that. How did you find the cookies?"

I studied Mrs. Jones, a serious-looking woman who appeared to be in her early sixties. She was wearing a red dress with white polka dots. Her expression was friendly, but

I wasn't sure if that welcoming friendliness extended to her daughter.

In fact, I didn't like the little dig she had made. Hallie was indecisive, but she wasn't stupid or incompetent.

"Oh, the cookies were fantastic, Mrs. Jones," I said. "Thank you for your hospitality. It's nice to be able to tell you so in person."

"You're welcome, honey! And I so appreciate you coming to help today!"

I chuckled. "It is so different here than in Atlanta."

"I can imagine. I hate to cut this short, Dr. Beckett, but I have to head inside and start on supper. Hallie's in the garage working on the float. She should be able to give you some guidance on what we're doing!"

I looked in the Jones' garage and spotted Hallie, looking as good as ever as she applied paint to the float. I smiled at Mrs. Jones.

"That sounds perfect."

"Nice to finally meet you, Dr. Beckett!" Mrs. Jones called as she began walking away.

"Luke," I replied absentmindedly.

My focus was locked on Hallie. My body was already moving toward her as I spoke. It was like it had a mind of its own.

Hallie was alone in the garage, and she didn't notice me as I entered the space. I stood as close to her from behind as I could and lowered my voice to speak.

"Never again, huh?"

Her spine straightened in surprise, but she was good at staying composed. She pulled the paintbrush away from the peach she was painting and turned just enough to catch my eye. There was a sexy glare on her face, and I chuckled.

"That's right," she hissed, her voice barely above a whisper. "And could you not talk about that right now? My mother's in the front yard."

"Oh, I ran into her. She just went inside to cook dinner. So... technically, not an issue."

Relief flooded Hallie's face, and I couldn't help but chuckle.

"Still, could you just drop it? I meant what I said. It's not happening."

"Not happening," I acknowledged, though my tone probably sounded as unconvinced as I was.

"Exactly. So like... let it go. And while you're here, could you maybe hold the corner of the paper up? I need to paint it but there wasn't enough glue on it so it fell down."

I scanned the float for a moment and located the spot Hallie meant. I remained close behind her, reaching an arm up over her shoulder to hold the paper in place. I could feel her response to me right in my bones.

"Sure, I'll let it go."

I spoke close to her ear and saw her tremor for a moment. Her body language was saying the exact opposite of her words, but I would let her play her little game. It made it all the more satisfying when I won.

"Perfect. Thanks."

She began to paint, inching a little further away from me. I decided that I would give her a little space and took a step to the left as she worked. I may have known how full of shit she was, but that didn't mean I had to make her uncomfortable.

"No problem."

There was a brief, charged silence before Hallie looked up at me. "So, how are you liking Peachwood?"

Was this her attempt at a normal, neighborly conversation? If so, I had to laugh. Still, if she wanted to pretend like I hadn't jizzed on her stomach a week ago, I could do that.

"It's... kind of a fishbowl," I stated. "Everyone knows all about me before I meet them. And people here are set in their ways. I'm not a fan of small thinking."

Hallie looked away. I expected her to be offended, but when she looked back, she was trying not to laugh. "You should meet my parents."

"One down, one to go."

Hallie rolled her eyes. "They were high school sweethearts. Very conservative and traditional. It's kind of a theme here. But it has its nice qualities."

"Oh, yeah... a very charming fishbowl," I teased.

"If you don't want to live here, why did you bother finding a job here?"

"If you don't plan on doing anything with your already useless degree, why did you get it?" I countered. "You work at a hardware store."

Hallie prickled. "I'm only working at that hardware store to make them happy. They want me to live this cookie-cutter life, just like them."

"What do you want? You're wasting your life working at a hardware store if it isn't what you really want to do. You realize that, right?"

Was I overstepping? Probably. Did I care?

Not one bit.

Hallie tensed for a moment before speaking. "Don't worry about what I'm doing for my career. I have my own thing in mind."

"Is that right? Because it looks to me like you're clueless and working in your parents' store and sitting on a useless degree." I could admit she was gorgeous. She'd even given me the best sex of my life. But it seemed clear to me that she was also a bit immature and unfocused.

Hallie set her jaw. "Like I said. I'm doing it for them right now, while I figure things out."

"Might want to get a move on or you'll be stuck in Peachwood selling screws for the rest of your life," I pointed out. The thing is, I wasn't even trying to be mean. She was floundering and if she didn't figure things out soon, life would only get harder.

"Well, I love Peachwood. I really do. But I want to do something I'm passionate about," she said. I could tell I was irritating her.

"Like?" I couldn't help prodding again. It was hard to believe she actually had something in mind.

"I already said that's none of your business. I'm a lot more than what everyone expects of me." She looked at me and I didn't say anything. "I get so much pressure from all sides. I guess that's what happens when you're a 'miracle baby.'"

"A miracle baby?"

"They had been trying to have kids for a long time before I was born," Hallie said, dipping her paintbrush into a canister of dark-blue paint. "They'd just about given up when my mom got pregnant. I was their last chance at being a real family. Now, they have a pretty narrow idea of how that's supposed to look."

"You can't blame them for being skeptical about your degree," I stated. "We've already established that it's useless."

Hallie glared at me, and I bit back a smile. There was nothing quite as satisfying as making her respond to me, even if it was in annoyance.

"I think everyone is too closed-minded about all that. It scares them to try to believe anything could exist other than what they've seen work for them. It seems you might be the same way. You should have no issue with fitting right in here."

Now it was my turn to prickle. "Let's not go that far," I said. "I may be set in my ways, but I'm certainly far from a stick in the mud."

Hallie's beautiful green eyes glittered when she looked at me. "Keep telling yourself that, pal."

I scoffed and Hallie laughed. We finished our work quietly. When we were done with the painting, I gave her a nod.

"See you later."

She hesitated before replying. "Yeah. See you later."

∼

I hadn't been sure what to make of my interaction with Hallie, but I didn't have a whole lot of time to think about it. The next day, I was back at work. It demanded all my attention and focus.

At the end of my shift, I was mentally exhausted but physically wired. I really needed a way to unwind. It was nice when I ran into Dr. Finley, the neurosurgeon, just before I left.

"Dr. Beckett, how are you?"

He greeted me with a warm and friendly smile. I couldn't help but return it. I took his offered hand to shake it.

"I'm great, how are you?"

He squinted at me as if appraising my truthfulness. "I'm well, thanks! But it's been a hell of a week. I was wondering if you'd like to join me and a few of my colleagues for drinks tonight. It would be good for you to meet people other than our local Casanovas."

I chuckled at the reference to Dr. Brian and Sam. Those two were always on the prowl. It seemed mostly harmless, but Dr. Finley wasn't wrong.

"Sure, I could use a drink," I replied.

This would be just the thing I needed to unwind after a grueling day. I loved my job, but it had an intensity that could leave my mind reeling for hours. It would be nice to sit back and relax in good company.

"No problem! I was going to shower and change here, then head out if you're up for it. Otherwise, I can send you the details."

I grinned. "Nah, I'll wait outside. Meet you by the cars."

Dr. Finley nodded and headed to the showers. I'd already gotten washed up and changed, so I waited by my car and toyed with my phone. He waved when he exited the building and came toward me.

"I'm not sure if you're familiar with the Outpost. It's a new bar in town. It's quickly becoming a favorite of ours," he said as he approached.

"I haven't heard of it."

"I'm sure it will pale in comparison to the places in Atlanta that you're used to, but we like it. You can follow me in your car if you like and I will show you the way."

"Perfect."

It didn't take long to drive across Peachwood. I followed him until he parked in front of a building with wood siding. We headed inside to find a table. It looked more like a lodge than a bar, but the ambience was comfortable.

"Ryder!" A muscular man with dark hair and blue eyes waved as he called Dr. Finley's name.

Ryder walked over and I followed, taking a look at the table. Another man was sitting at it with a pitcher of beer. He was lean, with friendly green eyes and dark brown hair.

"Hey, Ryder," he said. "And, uh..."

He regarded me as if trying to remember whether or not we had already met. I stepped forward to fill in the gaps.

"I'm Luke Beckett," I said, offering a hand. "A pleasure to meet you."

"Likewise. Max Ledger," he said, taking my hand with a firm pump.

"Luke works in the ER. A new recruit! I figured I'd introduce you all before Sam and Ollie decide he's one of them."

"Good call," the man who was standing said, turning to face me. He smiled and offered his hand. "You really don't want one of their matching T-shirts. They're kind of lewd."

I chuckled and shook his hand. "I believe you."

"Barrett Finley, by the way."

"My cousin," Ryder stated.

I nodded in acknowledgment. "Nice to meet you all. Thanks for the invite."

Barrett nodded with a friendly smile. "Take a load off, you two. Didn't your shifts just end? And help yourselves to the beer. It's the best in the county."

We all settled in at the table and started chatting casually. Ryder smiled at his cousin.

"How's the family?"

Barrett lit up. "Sage is as beautiful as ever. And she's such a good mom. Our kids are so lucky. I'm so lucky."

"Is Eden still loving being a big sister?"

Barrett laughed in a low baritone. "Oh, she does most of the time. She has little bossy moments with him here or there, but there's not much she can say to a six-month-old to hurt his feelings."

We all chuckled.

"Wait until he's old enough to walk," Ryder said. "I bet that will be a whole different ball game."

"Oh, I'm sure it will," Barrett said, his infectious laugh bringing a smile to my lips. "But she's such a sweet little girl. I'm sure they will be close."

"Yeah, she's a great kid."

"Do you want to see her holding him?" Barrett asked. He pulled out his phone and began going through several photos of his family.

I listened as the guys went into deep conversations about their families. I didn't have anything to contribute, but I was happy to listen. Considering my luck with women, I probably never would.

But there was more to life than having your heart ripped out of your chest. I was over it.

"Penny and I have been busy with the remodel of our house," Max said, glancing up from his phone. He had been texting with his wife off and on since we'd arrived. "And she's happy that you're working at the hospital now, Luke. I told her you seem like a good guy."

"And he's great at his job," Ryder confirmed.

Max smiled, then continued typing away to his wife. He was still pretty good at carrying on a conversation, even though it was clear that his wife was his top priority. I expected that we would all be drinking together until late into the night.

I was surprised when Barrett stood. "I've got to head out. I promised to help Sage put Caleb to bed. It's like my dad said, the first rule of marriage is making your wife happy."

Barrett shook my hand. "Welcome to Peachwood, Luke. I'm sure I'll see you around sometime."

"Thanks, man."

I felt a nagging sensation in the pit of my stomach. These guys didn't realize how lucky they were.

Or maybe they did. Either way, they had something really special. Something I didn't have a chance at.

I felt a twinge of sadness at the thought. I had been so unlucky with love that the idea of a family was laughable. It was something just out of my reach.

There was no use in crying over it though. Instead, I mustered my smile and lifted my glass of beer toward the other guys. "To escaping diaper duty," I said.

They laughed and lifted their glasses. The conversation carried on for another half hour before the others were also eager to get back to their wives and families. I finished my beer and left, trying not to focus on the fact that I would be going home alone.

CHAPTER 13

HALLIE

I really hadn't expected Luke to continue to work on the peach-themed float with me. But to my surprise, he kept on showing up. He also kept pissing me off.

I didn't think I had ever met a more arrogant man in my life. He was constantly poking fun at my life choices. It was like he thought he had it all figured out and I was just some lost little girl.

But I wasn't just a lost little girl. I was a grown woman who knew what she wanted. Whether he believed me or not was his own problem.

"Why are you taking this whole float thing so seriously, anyway?" he asked, leaning against the big peach and folding his arms over his chest. "It's just a silly parade."

"Unlike you, I like to show a little pride in the place I live," I said, squinting at him pointedly. He chuckled and shook his head as if I were, again, being a petulant child.

"Nothing says town pride more than a giant peach," he teased. I glowered at him.

"Hey, you're the one who's out here working on it. Maybe

I'd be getting more done if you'd spend more time helping and less time putting me down."

"I'm not putting you down," he said, sounding genuinely surprised. I huffed and rolled my eyes.

"Sure, you're not."

"Anyway, you're acting a little more manic this week is all. I was just curious what got into you."

My mind wandered back a couple of days. I had been working at the hardware store when who should wander in but Penny and Max Ledger. They were there to buy supplies for their float. They lived on Mulberry Lane, and they showed me pictures of their progress.

It looked so good that a fierce competitive streak flared up in me. I wanted to make sure that Peach Tree Lane would have the representation it deserved. I wanted to show pride in the place where I lived.

"There's nothing manic about taking pride in your work, *Luke*," I said. "I would have assumed you knew that, being a superior ER doctor and all."

He chuckled and shook his head at me. Why was he so damn condescending?

"Maybe you'd be better off putting some of that enthusiasm into doing something constructive for your future," he said. "This is fleeting. What you do with yourself will count for the rest of your life."

I rolled my eyes. I was sorely tempted to let him know just how wrong he was about me. In fact, I have been working a lot on my novel lately. I was feeling very good about it.

The idea of telling him that I wanted to be a romance author made me cringe, though. He didn't need to know a thing about it. He would just make fun of me for it the way he made fun of everything else.

"My life is my own to worry about. Man, between you and my parents, I just don't get a break," I grumbled.

I moved further away from Luke to work on a part of the float that he wasn't near. I could hear him laughing at me as I did.

If I could have stomped off entirely, I would have. But after seeing how beautiful Mulberry Lane's float was, I just couldn't bring myself to leave. I wanted to make this count.

"Yeah, yeah. I understand. You'd rather try to convince yourself that you're not aimless by putting extra effort into things that barely matter."

"I'm not listening. Peach Tree Lane will not be outdone!"

He chuckled and turned away. "Well. I will leave you to your very important task. I have some errands to run."

"Cool. You should probably go do your very important errands." *And leave me the hell alone.*

But I didn't say that part.

He shook his head at me again. Thankfully, I couldn't see the mirthful glint in his blue eyes this time. He was already walking away.

Good riddance.

I used the fuel from my annoyance to get a lot of work done on the float. When I glanced at my watch, I was surprised. Two hours had passed, and I had to go.

I had a novel to write.

"I'm so glad you made it, Hallie!"

I couldn't help but beam at Whitney as she opened the front door to her house and ushered me inside.

She gave me a big hug. She had invited me to the barbeque in one of her many attempts to socialize me. It had been so long since I'd lived in Peachwood that she had taken it upon herself to help.

Which was absolutely typical of her. When I was six, and Whitney was thirteen, she had been my babysitter. She had always been protective of me.

Now that we were both adults, it hadn't changed at all. She was always looking out for me. I was so grateful for her kindness.

"Thank you for inviting me, Whit. It's nice to be back. It feels like it's been ages since I've seen everyone."

"It has," Whitney said with a smile. She ran her hands through her sun-kissed brown hair. She'd gotten a bit tan already, making the freckles on her nose more apparent. "Four years away from home is a really long time."

"Sometimes it almost doesn't feel like long enough, but at the same time it was like an eternity."

She laughed brightly, her eyes sparkling. "I can totally understand that. I love our town, but sometimes I also love the idea of taking a nice long vacation."

"Definitely."

"Come on. I need to prepare a few things, and then we can go to the back. That's where everyone is gathered."

"Sounds great!"

Whitney led me into the house, smiling at a few random guests who were mingling in the living room area talking as preparations were made. A sudden, familiar voice made me freeze.

"Yeah, it's going really well, thank you."

Luke.

I grimaced but had to quickly change my expression. Whitney was looking at me now. What the hell was Dr. Arrogant doing here?

"Have you met Dr. Beckett?"

"Yeah, I have," I muttered.

Whitney looked out the window toward the grill in the backyard. "Oh, gosh," she said, looking in the direction of Ryder, her husband. He was standing there flipping burgers. A perfectly ordinary scene. Whitney's sudden change of tone seemed out of place. "It looks like Ryder needs a little help with the grill. Would you and Luke mind fixing the salad for me?"

"Uh…" I hedged.

"Of course," Luke interjected.

Of course.

"Great! I owe you two!"

I watched as Whitney disappeared into the yard, leaving Luke and me alone in the kitchen.

"Hallie," he said with a courteous nod. But there was a mischievous glint in his eye that I didn't appreciate.

"Luke," I grumbled, looking around for a knife.

The ingredients for the salad were all laid out on the counter already. I looked out the window for Whitney again with a distinct note of grumpiness. It felt almost like she had set the whole thing up.

Ryder was perfectly capable of manning the grill on his own. In fact, they were just standing there laughing. Yes, this was definitely a setup.

"What's the matter? Never made a salad before?" Luke asked, taking my hesitation the wrong way. Because of course he would.

"Of course I've made a salad before," I snapped, biting my tongue so I wouldn't add, *you jerk.* Instead, I restrained myself with, "I've made a lot of different kinds of salads. Some salads you might not have even heard of!"

"Is that right?" he asked with a teasing lilt in his voice.

I didn't answer and instead began chopping. He snickered and joined in beside me. I tried to ignore him, even though I could feel myself drawn to him.

My body was *such* a traitor.

This guy was the biggest asshole on planet Earth. Arrogance incarnate.

And here I was, fiending for him like an addict. I hated it. What was wrong with me?

"So. Have you gotten your life in order yet, or are you still blowing around like a leaf in the wind?"

"I'm not a leaf! And there's no wind."

I seethed, chopping faster. Luke chuckled. "I'll take that as a no."

I was so tempted to spill everything about my novel. I'd been making really good progress with it. If I could get it published, there would be a lot of potential in it.

But I couldn't tell Luke that. In fact, the only person I'd let read it was Tamara. She'd been obsessed with it, so I often sent her updates on my progress.

It kept me going to know that she loved it so much. But I had a feeling Luke wouldn't be impressed by a budding romance novelist. He had his own idea of who I should be.

And I didn't like it.

"I don't know why you're so obsessed over what I do with my life when it literally has no effect on you whatsoever," I said.

I tried not to talk with my hands, considering I was holding a knife. He already thought I was aimless. He didn't need to think I was a serial killer.

"I don't like to see wasted potential. And you're wasting your potential."

"I didn't ask you," I stated. I finished chopping and began placing everything in the large bowl that Whitney had set out. He chuckled.

"Unsolicited advice is one of my specialties," he said.

"I noticed. And it's gross," I stated. I tossed the salad quickly and grabbed the big bowl.

DOCTOR'S SECRET TWINS

I could feel Luke's eyes on me as I stalked away and headed to the backyard. Several more people were gathered outside. I set the salad down next to the big plate of hamburger buns on the table near the grill.

I plastered a smile on my face and tried to regain my composure.

Luke Beckett got under my skin more than anything I'd ever known. Why did I bother talking to him?

Sure, he was sexy as hell. He made my body feel things that I didn't even know were possible. But just because he was good in bed didn't mean he was good company.

He was awful company, in fact. Dr. Arrogant was someone I was just going to have to live without. He did nothing but piss me off.

Well, except he *also* gave me amazing orgasms. But those were negligible. I could survive without great sex.

"Hallie! Over here!"

I was distracted from my thoughts by the sound of Penny's voice. I smiled over at her. She was standing up at a big picnic table and waving her arms for me to join her.

Penny had moved to Peachwood while I was in New York. But she and her husband, Max, were regulars at the hardware store these days. They were remodeling a gorgeous historic Victorian house.

"Hey, Penny!" I grinned as I walked over.

She pulled me into a warm hug. Her blonde hair was wrapped in a loose bun. Like Whitney, who was now sitting at the table with her, her freckles had popped with the summer sun. Next to Whitney was beautiful Sage, who wore her long dark hair in loose waves.

Sage offered me a warm smile. "Hey, sunshine," she said, patting the bench beside her. She was holding her baby, Caleb. Sage was another newcomer to Peachwood, but

Whitney had introduced us since I'd been back in town. This was my first time meeting her six-month-old son.

"Hi, Sage. Hi, Caleb."

I sat down and leaned in to her for a half hug.

"You want to hold him?" she asked.

"Sure, okay."

I took the chubby baby in my arms, careful to support his head.

Whitney laughed. "You look good with a baby in your arms, kiddo."

I chuckled, studying the infant's perfect face.

Whitney sighed. "It's good to have you back in town, Hallie. I missed you."

I smiled. "I missed you, too. Seriously, it's been so long!" The baby was getting fussy, so I handed Caleb back to Sage.

A little girl ran across the yard, laughing as Barrett chased her. I had to look twice. I blinked at Sage. "Was that Eden?"

"Yes, if you can believe it!" Sage laughed.

I shook my head. "I just met the kid last week, and she's already like a foot taller."

"She's going through a growth spurt. I can't keep up with her."

"And now you've got this guy, too," Penny said.

"Yeah, these two keep me pretty busy, but I wouldn't change a thing."

I smiled at her. She looked so happy that I couldn't help but feel warm inside. It seemed like she had it all.

"I'm really glad," I said. "I think motherhood agrees with you. You're glowing."

"Glowing?" Penny asked, turning to study Sage. "Are you pregnant again?"

We all broke out into laughter and Sage shook her head. "No, no. Not yet."

"If you say so," Penny replied with a slight shrug. "But I'm keeping an eye on you."

"If you think that you have it in you to keep Barrett off me, be my guest. But good luck trying."

We all laughed again. Ryder walked up carrying Skye, who was an angelic little dark-haired one-year-old.

"She wants her mommy," Ryder said, passing Skye to Whitney.

"Come here, baby." Whitney took the squirming girl into her arms and cuddled her.

It seemed like everyone was having kids all of a sudden. But I had to admit, the young families I knew seemed pretty happy.

"Did you and Luke finish the salad?" Whitney asked with a gleam in her eyes when Penny and Sage were chatting about Caleb's facial features.

"Yes, and I don't appreciate your little ploy," I muttered under my breath.

"What ploy?" Whitney blinked, but a smile tugged at her lips.

I narrowed my eyes at her, then we broke out in laughter.

"Luke's not half bad, you know," Whitney said.

I rolled my eyes. "You obviously don't know him very well."

Whitney laughed. "You sound like you speak from experience."

I grabbed a beer, hiding my face. I didn't want to comment on *that*.

I chatted with my friends as we gorged ourselves on burgers and hot dogs. Then I called it a night. I was still a little off after Luke's latest lecture—and my body's betrayal.

By the time I left the barbeque, one thing was clear in my mind.

Dr. Arrogant had to go.

CHAPTER 14

LUKE

I glanced at my watch, cursing under my breath. I was at work when I was supposed to have the day off. But that was the risk of a job like mine.

You can't gamble with lives. No matter how much you want to see your sexy neighbor's smug face when she watches her corny float pass in the parade.

Still, it was irritating to know that if I was at work too late, I would end up missing it. I'd worked beside her on the silly float all this time. Now I couldn't even reap the reward for it.

I'd been hoping to lure her to my bedroom after the parade and the city fireworks display. I'd been craving her badly, but she had been acting distant lately. I knew it was probably because I'd been ribbing on her too much.

That wasn't a big deal to me, but maybe she was sensitive about it. I could lay off for a while if I had to.

After all, I didn't want to hurt her.

But it wouldn't kill her to listen to some constructive advice. Life was passing her by. She could have been well on her way through grad school by now.

Instead, she was miserable working at her parents' hardware store. And she could end up being stuck there for the rest of her life. I knew how small towns worked.

"Luke, how are you doing?" I turned to find Dr. Max Ledger standing behind me with a clipboard and a friendly smile.

"Great," I said, returning the smile. "How are you?"

"Well. Good but kind of in a hurry. I wanted to join Penny at the parade tonight."

"Penny… why does that name sound familiar?"

"I'm pretty sure she sold you your house."

The dumbfounded expression on my face must have shown. Max started laughing.

"I'm officially part of the fishbowl," I murmured.

"I have a sticker for that in my office. I could go get it for you if you want." Max offered a charming grin.

I snorted and shook my head. "Nah, I'm good."

"Speaking of small-town fishbowls, are you going to the parade tonight? The Fourth of July is kind of a huge deal around here." Max chuckled. "In case you couldn't tell by the way everyone is obsessed with their neighborhood floats."

"I did, actually, notice the float obsession," I admitted.

"You worked on one, didn't you?" Max's tone was accusing, but in a teasing way.

"I'm afraid so."

"Interesting. Very interesting."

"Yeah, yeah," I said, waving him off. "I'm sure you worked on one too."

"Oh, yeah. Religiously. I didn't have much of an option on that one."

"Why's that?"

Max grinned. "My wife insisted. She got really into the whole thing this year. And, well, every year since I've known her, really."

"How'd it turn out?"

"Really well! I'm supposed to head out soon so I don't miss it when it goes by. Penny will divorce me if I miss this. She loves all this cutesy small-town stuff."

I thought of Hallie and wondered if she would be upset if I ended up missing our float because of work. But that was a silly thought. Just because she had worked on it with me, it didn't mean she wanted to watch it go by with me.

Even though I wanted to watch it with her.

I brought my attention back to Max. "You don't like the small-town stuff?"

"Well… I'm also originally from Atlanta, so it's not quite as dazzling to me as it might be to someone more local."

I chuckled. "I can relate."

"I figured," Max said with a grin. "It took me a while to adapt to the small-town lifestyle. Not that it's bad, really. It's just very different."

"It really is. I'm not sure I'm quite as adaptable."

Max chuckled. "Give it time. And maybe a special woman. Anything is possible with that combination."

I was skeptical on that one but decided not to say anything about it. Instead, I smiled. "So what brings you to my neck of the woods of Lakeview Hospital? Anything I can help with?"

Max shook his head and held up the clipboard briefly. "I'm just here to check on a patient. A cardiologist's work is never done."

I smiled. "That's the truth."

"Are you planning on going to the parade?"

I glanced at my watch again. "That kind of depends on how the rest of my shift goes. I think I might be able to make it if I finish my rounds in the next hour."

"Ah, there's nothing quite as satisfying as seeing the Peachwood locals roll by as they pelt candy at you."

I snorted. "I'm sure it will be a highlight of my time here."

"Absolutely." Max checked his watch and smiled. "Well, I've got to get going! Cardiology and the threat of divorce beckon." He chuckled. I sensed there was no risk of him and Penny divorcing. "I'll see you there, maybe."

I grinned at Max, and he continued on his way to his patient. I decided to hustle and got my rounds done a little bit early. The traffic was horrible, though, because of the holiday.

By the time I drove down to where the Independence Day Parade was being held, I was sure I would miss it. I was relieved to see that the parade hadn't quite ended yet. I scanned the crowd and locked my eyes on Hallie.

She was as beautiful as ever. She wore another tempting tank top and a pair of khaki shorts. Her form was mesmerizing.

I watched her from a distance for a moment. She was smiling and waving at a little girl on a float. I squinted and recognized her as Barrett's daughter, Eden.

The little girl was trying her hardest to throw an armful of candy to Hallie, who was exaggerating her efforts to catch it. I couldn't repress my own smile.

The whole thing was annoyingly cute. I made my way to her and greeted her with a smile. I was surprised when her face fell.

"You almost missed the whole parade," she muttered.

"I think you're exaggerating," I said, my tone calm and even.

She pouted at me and looked away. It was an expression I hadn't known I loved so much until I saw it.

"No, I'm not. You could have missed our float. Look, it's coming."

I leaned over her shoulder to look. My chest pressed

against her back, and I felt her tense up against me. "So it is," I said.

She gave a small grunt in reply. I was still pressed against her and couldn't help but lean close to her ear. "I want you. Tonight. Come to my house after the parade is over."

She shivered slightly against me. I could feel my whole body respond to it. "That wouldn't be a good idea."

"No?" I continued. "Because I bet you won't be able to make it halfway through the fireworks before you're in my bedroom."

I pulled away as she shivered again. I could tell that I was leaving her body wanting for me the way mine was wanting for her. I wasn't even sorry about it.

I stepped back and watched our float go by. I knew Hallie was proud of it, but all I could think about was how good it was going to feel to fuck her again.

On the plus side, I was confident in my own words. Hallie might be grumpy at me, but she still wanted me. And before the night was over, I would have her again.

CHAPTER 15

HALLIE

"Just one beer. Then I really should go."

I knew I was lying to myself. In fact, I couldn't have cared less about the beer. Ever since I'd felt Luke against me at the parade, there had been only one thing on my mind.

Damn him. Why did that cocky smile of his do so much for me? I literally couldn't help myself.

"You got it," Luke replied. He disappeared into the kitchen and returned with two beers already uncapped. He offered one to me. "Your float was quite a hit."

"*Our* float," I corrected. "I didn't make it all by myself. It belongs to you too. And the whole neighborhood."

Luke chuckled and took a swig of his beer. "Right. Our float, then. It was nice. The parade I mean."

"Yeah..."

I hesitated to ask what was burning on my mind. Why hadn't he been there sooner? I hadn't realized how much I wanted to be able to enjoy the parade with him.

Not that I gave a damn about *that*, but he'd worked on the

float after all. It seemed kind of rude to just miss the whole purpose of it. I decided I would ask.

"Why were you so late?"

Luke caught my eye. I felt my heart surge with a strange feeling. I wanted to look away but couldn't.

"They called me in to work. I planned on being there sooner."

"Oh."

I didn't really know what else to say about that. It made me feel a little better for some reason. He wanted to be there.

I was being silly, though. He was still an asshole, even if he wanted to watch the parade. It didn't automatically make him a good guy.

"I owe you an apology."

I frowned as I tried to figure out which of the million things he'd be apologizing for. But when his lips curled, I knew not to get my hopes up. It was a scam, even if the smile made me weak in the knees. "For what?"

Might as well play along, right?

"I was wrong. You made it through the whole fireworks display. I'm impressed."

I rolled my eyes, and his irritatingly sexy grin grew bigger. "Just because you think I'm a slave to your cock doesn't mean I am."

"Of course," he said with a patronizing nod. "You're just here for my amazing company."

I sighed and set my beer down. "I don't have to be," I warned.

I began to turn toward the door when Luke's hands were on my hips from behind. I gasped when I felt him hard against my ass. A fire that only he seemed to stoke in me suddenly consumed my entire body.

I sighed as I felt his lips drop against my neck. His kisses sent a soft fire down my spine. I closed my eyes and leaned back against him.

His hands began to roam up and down my body. All thoughts of leaving left my mind. All I wanted was him.

Luke turned me around gently so I was facing him. He surprised me with a deep, almost tender kiss. I gripped his shoulders and got lost in it. He was a really good kisser.

Just as his hands had roamed my body, mine began to roam his. I appreciated his six-pack with my fingers. Then I let my hands trail down his abdomen and rest on his belt buckle.

He took a sharp intake of breath as I undid it with one hand. My other stroked over his hard member. I had a sudden urge to feel more of it.

When I was finished unbuckling him, I let his jeans drop to the floor. He raised a brow at me as if making sure I knew what I was doing. I gave him a smile before dropping to my knees.

I pulled his boxers down, then heard him moan as I took him into my mouth. I ran my tongue up and down his shaft, teasing it a little before submerging it entirely in my mouth's heat. He began to run his hands through my hair.

He was huge. Bigger than any man that I had ever seen. Which wasn't saying much considering my experience, but still.

I tried to give him head as good as he had consistently given me. Apparently, it was working. His fingers tightened around my hair and he groaned again, moving his hips slightly. I began to bob my head to keep up with him, taking him in as deeply as I could to pleasure him.

"Fuck," he whispered as I began choking on his cock. He stilled and then picked me up from my kneeling position.

He bent me over the kitchen counter. I could feel myself

physically responding to him in preparation. It was almost irritating how much I wanted him.

"I have condoms this time," he said, bending down to grab his wallet from the jeans he'd stepped out of. I heard him put the condom on.

I gasped in pleasant surprise when I felt his shaft rubbing against my clit. He was readying himself to enter. I couldn't have wanted it more.

He teased me for several more seconds before finally I felt pressure against my opening. He started slowly at first.

Then he seemed to realize that I was fully ready, and my body was shocked by the mass of his cock pushing into me. I let out a loud cry of pleasure and he began to thrust.

It was a slow pace at first. Almost as if he wanted to relish it. But soon, he began to pick up speed.

I braced myself against the counter, my body writhing with bliss. It had been way too long since he'd fucked me. I'd almost forgotten just how good it felt.

As if to remind me, he reached his hand around my body. His skillful fingers began to circle my clit. It enhanced my pleasure so much that I bowed my head and gasped.

He let out a grunt of approval and his body continued to thrust. Harder and deeper until I was all but begging to come. He was teasing me this time though, and I already knew why.

He wanted us to come together again.

As if to confirm my suspicions, he picked me up and carried me into his bedroom. It made me feel self-conscious at first, like he had full control of me. But for some reason, it was sexy with Luke.

He sat down on the bed and held me in his lap as he lay back. His hands guided my hips to his cock again. I slid down on it, knowing exactly what he wanted.

He groaned, his hands tightening around my waist as I

began to thrust my hips. He urged me on with his hands, still thrusting his hips beneath me. I couldn't help but moan as wave after wave of euphoria traveled through my bloodstream.

I began to pick up the pace. I was dangerously close to coming, but I wanted the same thing Luke did. I'd never been so connected with someone else's body before.

He let out a low groan and I could sense that he was close now. I went wild, grinding against him as fast as I could. He arched back into the pillows, his face taut with pleasure.

Finally, I couldn't help myself. I could feel the hot electricity swimming in my abdomen. My release began, and I tightened around his cock as I came. He groaned in pleasure, gripping my hips and making up for the slowness of my pace.

He carried me through my climax that way as he finally unleashed his load. I came harder than I had ever come in my life. My body was shaking by the time my climax was finished, and he pulled me down against him.

I rolled to the side of the bed beside him, but it felt good to be against his chest that way. I shivered and snuggled up a little closer to him.

"I'm cuddling with you because it's cold in here. Not because I particularly want to," I announced. "Just for the record."

He laughed. "Noted."

"Do you have to keep your room at negative seven degrees?" I complained. He chuckled and wrapped an arm around me, pulling me close to him.

I allowed it reluctantly, resting against his chest. "Yes. It's July."

I rolled my eyes but enjoyed the deep baritone of his laughter through his chest. "Whatever you say."

"It's always cold at the hospital. Maybe I just got used to it."

"How come you decided to become a doctor? Was it really for the money?"

I don't know where the question came from. It seemed to surprise Luke, too. It surprised me even more that he was willing to answer it.

"No," he said. "Actually, I had a friend when I was a kid. He was sick all the time. And I guess I thought if I could help people who were struggling with health problems, it would make my life feel better. To give someone relief if they're hurting."

"Oh. That's actually... sweet." The last word was a little hard to say.

Luke shrugged and didn't speak for a moment. "I was thinking about being a surgeon, but then I had a moment where there was an emergency in an elevator. An old man had collapsed, and I gave him CPR. I realized that I wanted to be there for people when they need it the most. It takes a certain kind of person to stay calm in a crisis."

I looked up into his beautiful blue eyes. "And you can do that."

"I can do that."

I ran my hand along his chest as I snuggled tighter. "So how come you're in Peachwood? You still don't seem to like it that much."

He drew a deep breath and let it out slowly. "I had a bad breakup in Atlanta. My ex slept with a coworker of mine—a friend, really. It was just too much. I wanted to start over in a place without bad memories."

"She hooked up with your coworker? After you'd broken up, or..."

I couldn't help the probing questions. I was fascinated by him. For some strange, sick reason.

"Actually, she cheated on me with him while we were still a couple. Then after we broke up, I saw them together at a hospital party. Like they were rubbing salt in my wounds."

"Ouch."

"Right. I realized I couldn't live the way I was anymore. So I put out some job applications. Lakeview was the best option out of all the offers I got."

"It's definitely a good hospital," I acknowledged.

"It is. And they hired me on the spot. I even found this place on the same day. It was almost like it was fate, so I decided to try it out and see how it went."

"Now you're a small-town guy instead of a big-city guy," I teased.

Luke chuckled. "Something like that. You're going through a similar thing, aren't you? You were in the big city for four years. Now you've returned to your small-town roots."

"Yeah... something like that."

"Did you like New York?"

I smiled. "I really did. There's never a dull moment in the Big Apple. It was a great place to be independent for the first time. And it was so different from living in Peachwood. It opened my mind... All the different cultures and things to do."

"I bet it did. You went from the fishbowl to the ocean," Luke said with a laugh.

"Yeah, I guess so. Then back to the fishbowl."

"You really like living here better?"

I paused for thought, then nodded against his chest. "Yeah. I really do."

"Huh." He was quiet for a few moments. "It isn't the worst."

I chuckled. "It's not. There are great things about it."

"I mean, it's growing on me, I guess. I could get used to you country bumpkins yet."

I rolled my eyes with a smile. "Whatever. At least it's a good place to raise a family." I yawned and closed my eyes.

Luke was silent for a long moment. Finally, he spoke quietly.

"I don't think that's in the cards for me, honestly. I'm not the type to settle down. A wife and kids would just tie me down too much."

"Oh," I said sleepily. His words didn't sit right with me, but I was too tired to question why.

I found myself drifting off to a deep sleep in Luke's strong arms.

When I woke up the next morning, my body was swimming with nausea. I untangled myself from Luke and ran to the bathroom, afraid I was going to get sick right on his sheets. I ended up making it to the toilet, where I hurled my guts out.

I washed up a little, then went to find my clothes. I glanced at Luke, who was still sound asleep.

Did I have a stomach bug or something?

I was probably just having a reaction to the fact that I'd spent the night with Dr. Arrogant himself. Who could blame me for feeling sick about it?

I dressed quickly and hurried home. There was no reason to make a big deal of this. But there was no reason to stay, either.

Right?

CHAPTER 16

LUKE

The next few days after the parade were hectic. Then again, that was kind of my life. I worked long hours and didn't find much time for company.

I hadn't seen Hallie since the night we'd fallen asleep in my bed together. It was more because of my schedule than anything else, but I felt her absence this time. I guess I was worried that she might be freaking out a little bit about what had happened.

Imagine my surprise on day three when Hallie showed up in the emergency room. I noticed her checking into the front desk as I breezed past, reading a file.

I stopped in my tracks. "Hallie?"

"Shit." Hallie didn't seem happy to see me. I knew the look in her eyes. She was ready to bolt.

"What's the matter?" I asked, stepping closer to her. I ignored the fact that she looked like she was ready to run away and instead ushered her to a room. Ethical or not, she was my top priority now.

"I don't feel good," she said simply. "Maybe a flu or a

stomach bug... but much worse than any bug I've ever had in my life."

"I see."

I took possession of her chart on the way to the room. Once we arrived, I guided her to the bed. I studied her, but she avoided eye contact.

"What's going on, Hallie?" I asked, my tone as gentle as I could possibly make it. I couldn't help myself. I was worried about her.

Still avoiding my eye, she sighed. "I've been feeling really sick."

"Sick how?"

"My stomach. I've been really nauseated lately. And throwing up a lot."

"How long have you felt sick?"

"Since the morning after we... since July fifth."

I studied her thoughtfully for a few moments. Why did I feel guilty somehow? I hadn't made her sick.

"What kinds of things have you been eating?"

She sighed and screwed up her eyebrows. "I don't know. Not much. I don't have much of an appetite."

"Well, what did you eat before you got sick?"

"Just the regular picnic food before the parade, you know? Nothing special. And everyone else ate it, and no one else got sick from it."

"All right. Did you have a fever at all?"

Hallie shrugged miserably. "I don't know. I don't think so?"

I sighed. That wasn't very helpful. All I wanted to do was to get to the root of the problem so I could help her feel better. I hated that she was sick.

"Okay, Hallie, a nurse will be in shortly."

"You're going?"

I really didn't want to. At all. But I had a few other people to check while the nurses did what needed to be done for Hallie's tests.

"I'll be back soon," I said. "I'll take care of you. Don't worry."

She managed to catch my gaze for a moment before her eyes flickered back to the floor. "Thank you."

"Of course." I flipped through the chart briefly, then looked back to Hallie. "Before we do anything, we have a few things to rule out, okay? Do you think you can pee in a cup for me?"

Hallie blushed. "Fine."

I couldn't help but chuckle to myself. A strange time for modesty, but I supposed it couldn't be helped.

"All right. Like I said before, a nurse will be with you in a few minutes with everything you need and the instructions. She'll also draw some blood so we can take a look at everything. When I get the sample, I'll send it down to the lab for testing. I'll get back to you with the results the second I get them. I promise."

"You're going to be handling my pee cup?" Hallie asked, her tone horrified. I laughed outright then.

"Briefly. But don't worry. I will take very good care of it."

She rolled her eyes, but I could see the corners of her lips twitching into a tired smile. Not that she wanted to smile.

That made it all the better. Even sick, she was beautiful. I felt a protective heat surge through my body and left the room.

I stood outside the door for a moment, my mind working out all the possibilities of what could be affecting Hallie this way. None of them made me happy, but I comforted myself with the possibility of a simple stomach bug.

My pager went off, so I didn't dwell on my worries for

too long. I had an ER to run, so to speak, and had to get to my next patient.

I got swept up in my other duties for the next twenty minutes. The second the results were ready, though, I was on them like a hawk. When I read them, my stomach dropped in confusion.

It couldn't be. Could it?

I almost felt like I had to sit down, but I had promised Hallie that I would be right in with her when I had the results. Instead of taking a moment to collect myself, I went to her room, my stomach in knots.

"Luke? Are you okay?"

No, I was far from okay, but I really didn't quite know how to say it. My chest was tight as I looked at Hallie. She seemed small the way she was sitting, curled into herself like that.

"I got your results back," I said, clearing my throat.

I hadn't meant to alarm her or lack composure. It was strange for me when dealing with a patient.

Then again, this was a situation I'd never been in before. I don't think I'd ever felt more tense in my life. A million thoughts were racing through my mind, but I had to maintain my composure.

Hallie seemed concerned and scooched forward. Her beautiful brow grew knitted. "Is something wrong with me?"

I hesitated, clutching the papers with the results. "Not exactly"

Hallie's eyes narrowed. "What? Well, what is it then?"

I cleared my throat and gave a terse nod. "There's no mistake about it."

"About what, Luke?" Her eyes bored into me, and I swallowed hard.

There were so many things I wanted to say. Advice I was

supposed to give her. But all professional conduct had gone out the window.

I had to get it together.

"You've been nauseated because of morning sickness," I finally said, somehow managing to keep my voice from breaking. "Congratulations, Hallie. You're pregnant."

CHAPTER 17

HALLIE

Pregnant?

I felt like I was going to faint. I sat in stunned silence as the news sank in. The walls were closing in on me.

Oh, God.

Luke nodded. His expression was hard to read. "Yes."

My heart was racing as if I had just run a marathon. Now the nausea I was feeling was even more intense, but for a completely different reason. I couldn't believe what I was hearing.

What had I been thinking? I'd had sex with Luke that one time without protection. I was so *stupid.*

Why had I let my body take the lead on these things? I'd known the risks. But one overpowering moment of lust had thrown all logic out the window.

And Luke was a doctor! Wasn't he supposed to have known better?

Why would he care, though? It wasn't going to affect him at all.

Me, on the other hand... Well, I'd have to deal with it for

the rest of my life. I felt another pang of bitter nausea. How could I have let this happen?

Nurses were bustling around outside the doorway of my room. It felt like the entire town was within earshot of this conversation. It made me uncomfortable.

The last thing I wanted was anyone to know that Luke and I had been seeing each other. My private life was meant to stay that way. Especially now…

"Hallie?"

I looked up at Luke. My chest was burning. It took all I had not to break down and cry.

"Yeah?" I managed, though the word felt like stone in my mouth. I wasn't ready for any of this.

Luke looked pale, but otherwise composed. Was he really that afraid of having a family? It made me feel like the dumbest woman alive.

I waited for him to speak. When he did, his question came out just above a whisper. "Am I the father?"

I opened my mouth, ready to tell the truth, but a nurse walked into the room with discharge papers. She set them on the table beside me. A sudden spike of panic consumed me.

I couldn't tell him the truth. He came into the room looking as if he had seen a ghost. He was *terrified* of the truth.

"Looks like you're free to go now, Hallie," the nurse said, glancing at the papers. "Good luck and take care of yourself!"

Luke's question was still heavy in the air. I knew I should answer him, but I just couldn't. Instead, I grabbed the discharge papers and left the room without looking back.

I had to process everything that had happened. There would be time to talk to Luke about it all later. Right now, I needed some space.

I made my way to my car, my head swimming. I had never imagined something like this happening to me. I was in shock.

I sat in the car for a long time, trying to collect myself. My entire life was going to change, and I was terrified and overwhelmed.

A baby. I found myself pressing a hand against my abdomen. *My* baby.

A tender feeling overwhelmed me. I was going to be a mother. And I already loved the child inside me.

I'd always wanted a family. But the timing and situation were all wrong. God, what a mess.

It was crazy, but my attachment to the baby, the concept of motherhood… that part felt right. It was everything else that was hard to imagine dealing with. Life was so strange.

I needed to go somewhere. Do something. If I sat here too long worrying about it all, I was afraid I might never move again.

I started my car and began to drive. I would go to the strip mall in Marietta. It would give me something to do while I tried to process all of it.

When I got there, I found myself wandering to a shop full of baby things. It felt a little strange, but right.

My heart grew tender as I began to look around. I ran my hand along soft blankets and onesies. What would my baby look like wearing them?

I picked up an outfit that was yellow with a cute elephant on the front. I would have to dress a tiny human being in clothes just like that.

There were also several cribs and bassinets on display. I walked around, running my hand along the different textures.

A baby. I was really going to be a mother. I couldn't believe it.

I felt a brief spike of fear. I had no idea if I was ready for this. But I would have to be.

I was about to leave when my phone vibrated. I checked

and saw that Luke had texted. I didn't even read it and put my phone away.

I was so not ready to talk to him about any of this. It was already hard enough without imagining how he would react. I needed time to react myself without worrying about fending him off too.

But time wasn't something he wanted to give me. A few minutes later, my phone began to ring. I glanced at it in case it was my parents, but it was Luke.

I felt a spike of annoyance. Why couldn't he just leave me alone? It wasn't every day a woman discovered she was going to be a mother.

I ignored the call and turned my phone on silent. I just couldn't deal with him right now. I could already imagine his reaction, and I didn't need it.

Luke already thought I was nothing but an immature child. He had made that abundantly clear during my time with him. The last thing I needed was another lecture.

Besides, anything he was going to say would just hurt me. I already knew that he wasn't the kind of guy to want a family. He had said as much to me himself.

I didn't think I would be able to handle hearing him say it again. Especially now, when I was carrying his child. I wanted to protect it, and myself.

Telling Luke he was going to be a father was not going to do that. It would probably make him resent me. And the baby. I'd tell him, just not right now.

I wasn't going to put myself in that position. I was already feeling vulnerable. That level of rejection would just be too much right now.

So I ignored his calls and texts for the rest of the day.

I'd tell him soon. But today, I needed to be alone.

CHAPTER 18

LUKE

I set my phone down with a heavy sigh. Hallie still wasn't answering me. God, I couldn't believe it.

My chest was tight as I thought about all the possibilities. I could be a father. Or... Hallie could become a mother without me.

She had the world at her fingertips, really, a beautiful girl like that. Who knew how many other people she could be seeing? Of course, there was likely to be someone she was more serious about than she was about me.

I hated the thought. My blood boiled, actually, but what could I do? All I wanted was to talk to her, but she wasn't answering me.

I hated it.

Pregnant. I wished she wouldn't have left the hospital so abruptly. I had so many questions.

I was tempted to try calling again, but I thought it might be best to wait for now. She was probably embarrassed about getting knocked up and having me find out like that. If it was mine, she would have just said so.

DOCTOR'S SECRET TWINS

But she hadn't. She'd run off and avoided the question. Now she was avoiding me entirely.

I hadn't realized the power that she had to crush me until that moment. I'd been so worried about her, and then to realize that she was sick because of a pregnancy? God, what a roller coaster.

We would have had a lot to talk about if I was involved. We'd have to discuss what we were going to do about it all. And if maybe she'd want to raise it together if I was the father.

That was assuming she would ever speak to me again. The way she'd taken off once she got her discharge papers seemed to answer my question well enough. Still, what if I was the father?

She didn't have to run from me that way if I was. I could have offered my help. She barely had her shit together as it was, and I knew she was probably so scared.

The idea of being the father had actually elated me. I had never considered the possibility before, but truthfully, it was nice. I would have loved to be involved in her life and have my own family.

And it could have been just what Hallie needed to get focused. She needed direction, and being a mother would be just the thing to help her find it. I would have been happy to support her in that.

Another wave of crushing disappointment crashed over me. I had to be realistic. I couldn't be some moron who got his hopes up over something like this.

Hallie most likely wasn't carrying my child. She had run away. And she had been avoiding me like the plague. If she had been seeing someone else too, her reaction made a lot more sense.

I hated the stinging dejection at the thought. I knew we hadn't had a talk about being exclusive or anything, but I hadn't wanted anyone but her. The thought that she did just kind of hurt.

I didn't want it to hurt, though. In fact, I had done everything I could to keep her at arm's length emotionally. Even though there was a part of me that just couldn't get enough of her.

But she was young, and pretty girls like Hallie weren't meant to stay single. It made sense that she had someone she was a little more serious about. Someone closer to her age whom she got along with better.

I was probably way too old for her anyway. I'd just been a good time to her, and I would have to accept that. It was disappointing, but it happened.

It didn't make me feel any better about it, though. Actually, I felt a little used.

But I shouldn't have been surprised.

Getting involved with women had a tendency to disappoint me. I didn't realize I had expected more from Hallie, but I had. I only wished she would have been honest with me about seeing other guys.

It was hard to stay focused throughout the day. I was relieved to finally get home.

When I stepped out of my car, I noticed Mrs. Jones outside. She waved and walked over to the fence with a friendly smile.

"Good afternoon, Mrs. Jones," I said.

"Oh, please, call me Melanie," she said with a bright laugh.

I smiled at her, even though seeing her reminded me of the situation with her daughter and the feelings I was trying to escape. In short, it didn't feel that great. But it wasn't her fault.

"Melanie, then," I said, managing to keep the smile pasted on my face.

"I wanted to thank you personally for helping with the

DOCTOR'S SECRET TWINS

Fourth of July float this year," she said, leaning against the fence. "It means a lot to the people on Peach Tree Lane. And it was nice to see you getting involved with the community. People get wary when new neighbors keep too much to themselves."

I chuckled and managed not to say anything about the fishbowl mentality of her words. Even though I would have immediately said it to her daughter, just to see her try not to laugh. "I understand."

"That's why I had Hallie invite you to help out. I didn't want people alienating you because they might think you're not interested in the community."

"That's very considerate of you, Mrs. Jones. Uh, Melanie." Hallie sprung up in my mind again, and a sudden idea occurred to me. "How's Hallie, by the way? Is she working today at the hardware store? I was thinking of picking up a few things for my house."

"Oh, that girl. I don't know what to do with her. She was supposed to work, but she got a wild hair and decided to take off for the night. She's gone out of town, but she should be back tomorrow."

"Ah… she's certainly an interesting one. That's for sure," I said.

"Interesting, yes. I just wish she could try to find some stability," Mrs. Jones said.

"And a little direction wouldn't hurt either."

Melanie let out a sharp laugh. "Tell me about it! I worry so much about her. You wouldn't believe it."

"Oh, I imagine I'd have an inkling," I said with a chuckle.

"You know, her father has always had dreams of leaving the hardware store to her. I just don't understand why she would reject a career that has fallen right into her lap. Most people work hard to have something like this. But she just doesn't want any part of it."

"Maybe it's too stable for her," I joked.

Melanie laughed. "It must be. She doesn't know what she wants to do, but she doesn't want to do the one thing that would provide for her and make sure she had what she needs. I'll never understand."

We chatted for a few more minutes before I went inside. The conversation had sparked a strong urge to check on Hallie and make sure she was all right. Her mother had no idea she was pregnant, but I suspected that was exactly what had caused her 'wild hair.'

I got my phone and tried once again to give Hallie a call. Just like every other time I'd tried to get in touch with her, she didn't answer. In fact, I was going straight to voicemail now. It didn't feel great.

I set my phone down on the counter and stared at it for a few moments, lost in thought. Was it possible that the baby actually was mine? Was that why Hallie was being so evasive?

The question circled in my mind. I only wanted to check on her and make sure she was okay. Maybe I could even let her know that if I had fathered her child, we would figure it out.

Together.

CHAPTER 19

HALLIE

My mother hadn't seemed very happy when I called to let her know I wouldn't be coming to work—or home that night, for that matter. But I couldn't imagine being home right now.

Especially when *home* was right next door to Luke.

There was a nagging guilt that was bubbling in me. It was distracting, honestly, and I just wanted it to go away.

He was the one who didn't want a family. Not me.

Instead of going home and confronting everything, I spent more time exploring Marietta. There was just too much for me to figure out before I could face my parents. Or Luke.

Marietta was beautiful, though. I couldn't help myself when I saw another baby boutique not far from where I'd been planning to rent a hotel. I pulled in and wandered inside, my hand resting on my abdomen.

I looked around the shop for close to an hour. I ended up leaving with a couple of adorable gender-neutral outfits for newborns. Of course, I didn't yet know what the sex would be, so I settled on a few prints that would look adorable on either.

My favorite was a green onesie with safari animals on it. The idea of seeing my baby in these clothes made my heart swell.

A large part of me couldn't wait. The fact that I'd be a mother was something I was surprisingly okay with. I just wished Luke wasn't the father.

It would be different if he hadn't just told me a family wasn't in his cards. But he had. And now I couldn't have felt more alone in this if I tried.

In fact, the idea of doing all of this without him terrified me. I hadn't been this close to a panic attack since my final exams. And this was so much more intense.

After I was satisfied that there were no other shops I'd want to visit before I retired for the night, I checked in at my hotel. I just needed some time to breathe and figure things out. Somewhere I could process everything without having to pretend everything was okay or talk about things before I was ready.

I puttered around my hotel room for a while before pulling out my laptop. I had to do something productive with all that nervous energy. Otherwise, I was just going to fall apart.

Some research would be a good idea. If I was going to do this on my own, I might as well be prepared.

I explored several parenting websites, researching babies and pregnancy. I even found a place where I could download several eBooks on the topic.

It felt good to give myself access to information. It made things seem a little less scary. I only wished I wasn't so alone in it.

And somehow, I knew telling Luke the truth would leave me feeling even more alone than I did now.

I perused the list of OB/GYNs in Peachwood, knowing that I would have to book soon with one. I tried hard not to think of *another* specific doctor back home while I did. It didn't do any good, however. Soon, my phone lit up with a text from Luke.

I sighed and read it.

Hallie, I'm worried about you.

I hesitated for a moment before finally biting the bullet and texting him back. I knew I really needed to talk to him. It was just so scary.

I'll talk to you tomorrow. I'll stop by your place after your shift.

I sent the text quickly before I could change my mind.

The interaction was small, but it left me swimming with anxiety. I closed my laptop and decided to call Tamara. My best friend always seemed to help me feel better when things were hard.

"Hal!" she answered the call brightly.

"Hey, bestie."

"What's wrong?"

"Nothing." I sighed. She had always been good at reading me. "I mean. Kind of."

"Give me ten minutes. I'm coming to see you. And I'm bringing ice cream."

"Actually, I'm not at home, but you can still come and see me if you are up for a drive."

"Of course! Where are you?"

"Um. Marietta."

"What are you doing all the way out there, Hal?"

"I needed to get out of Peachwood for a while. I'll explain more when you get here."

"Okay. Hold tight and text me the address where you're at. I'll be there in a bit longer than ten minutes, but I will still have ice cream."

I laughed softly. "You're the best. Can't wait."

"*You're* the best! I'll see you soon."

We hung up, and I paced around the hotel room for a while until I finally got the text that Tamara was at the hotel. I went down and brought her up to the room with me. She set a pint of ice cream and a spoon on the table, and we sat down to talk.

"So. Tell me what's going on," she said, eyeing me up and down. "Something is definitely different with you."

"Yeah, you can say that again," I said with a sigh.

"What's happening, Hal?"

Tamara looked worried now, and I knew I would have to spill soon before I really put her through hell. She hated to see me upset, and it was the same with me toward her.

"Brace yourself, because I kind of have some news."

"Okay..."

A lump suddenly formed in my throat. I wasn't even sure I would be able to choke the words out. I had to say them, though.

"I'm pregnant."

Tamara sat in stunned silence for several seconds. "Pregnant?" she croaked.

I nodded. "Yep. I just found out a few hours ago."

"You... having a *baby*, Hallie?"

My hands went to my belly, and I nodded. "Yes."

Finally, a big smile creased her face. "No way! You mean I'm going to be an aunt?"

She wiggled excitedly in her seat, and I couldn't help but laugh through my tears. "You are. And you will be the best aunt my baby could ever hope for."

I felt a sense of peace in knowing I was speaking the truth. Tamara was a gentle soul, despite her boisterous ways. She would be so much fun and so supportive, both of my baby and me.

"Okay, so who's the dad?" she asked, blinking at me as she

tried to put the pieces together. "I didn't know you were seeing anyone! Spill!"

"I've been kind of keeping it to myself because I'm embarrassed about it," I admitted.

"What could you possibly have to be embarrassed about, Hal?" Tamara asked. "It's me! I would never judge you."

"I know, but I mean… he's kind of a jerk. And I know you'd judge *him*, even if you don't judge me. I just can't believe I like him so much. It's been really weird for me."

"Ah. I think I get that," Tamara said, nodding sagely. "So, who is he?"

"Remember that guy I met at the bar that night you were dancing with Paul?"

She rubbed her temples. "Vaguely. I had too many shots that night. I just remember you were awfully quiet about what happened when you left."

"Well, I hooked up with him. And he was good in bed. *Really* good. But he's annoying as hell every time he opens his mouth to speak."

"So, it was just the one time?"

I blushed. "No, there have been a couple other times. Once without a condom."

"Oh."

I rolled my eyes. "I know it was dumb. I should've known better. I should've stayed away from him. But something about the guy draws me to him like a magnet."

Tamara nodded. "I've been there. You're addicted to his cock."

"And his tongue," I muttered. "But he's an arrogant bastard. Likes to give me lectures about my future."

"You get enough of that from your parents." Tamara wrinkled her nose. "So, this guy is why you've been MIA the past two weeks?"

"Yeah. I'm sorry." I bit my lip.

She shrugged. "It's no big deal." She took my hand. "And now you're pregnant by the guy."

"Yeah… and the worst part is, I really don't think he wants to be a father," I said, my voice wavering. "He said it isn't in the cards for him to have a family."

Tamara winced. "Ouch. That makes things harder, then."

"A lot harder," I said with a sigh.

"Do you want him to be involved?"

I let myself think about the question. The truth was, I would have loved it if Luke had been more open to having a family. There was a part of me that might have been growing really attached to him, as much as I hated to admit it.

"It would be nice not to have to do this alone, but I don't want him to resent me or the baby. I don't know if I could handle that."

"I understand. What about child support?"

"I mean… he's a doctor, I'm sure he could afford it. But I hate the idea of going through all of that. I'd rather deal with it on my own."

"So, he just doesn't want anything to do with your pregnancy? He sounds like a piece of shit."

I prickled. My instinct was to protect Luke. "It's not that. I haven't told him about it yet."

"Well, there's time to figure out how you want to handle it."

I sighed. "Not really. He's the one who told me."

Tamara blinked at me in surprise. "Wow. And he didn't know it was his?"

"He asked me, but then a nurse came in the room before I could answer. I was so overwhelmed and confused, I just left after that. Then I drove up here and I've been ignoring his calls."

"Wow…"

"So… he might think he's not the father. But he texted me

a little while ago and said he was worried, so I told him I'd talk to him tomorrow when he gets off work."

Tamara blew out a deep breath. "Wow, Hal. That's a lot going on for you."

I laughed without humor. "Yeah, it really kind of is."

"So, are you going to tell him the baby is his when you guys talk?"

"I guess so. But I can't stand the thought of him rejecting us like that. It almost feels better if he doesn't have the choice to do what I already know he's going to do."

"Okay, but how do you know for sure that he's going to react the way you think he is?"

God, if only. But I couldn't let myself get my hopes up. I already had a pretty good idea of how this guy operated.

When it came to casual sex, he was the most pleasant and attentive he could possibly be. But with everything else, he was kind of an asshole. And he didn't try to hide it, either.

"He said he doesn't want to settle down."

If Luke said it, it meant he believed it. I knew that much by now.

"That doesn't mean he wouldn't want to know that he's a father," Tamara pointed out. "And feelings can change just like situations change. Nothing is set in stone."

I shifted in my seat. "I guess so..."

"I think you should at least give him the option to show up for you instead of assuming the worst," Tamara pointed out. "If he wants nothing to do with it, fine. You know he's the asshole you're afraid he's going to be. But he might surprise you."

I swallowed hard, unable to keep the tears from springing into my eyes. Tamara was right. I had to at least give him the option.

"I don't know," I whispered. "I'm scared to be disappointed."

"Oh, Hal," Tamara said, frowning sympathetically. "You never know. He might actually be happy about it! Or supportive. You won't know until you try. And when you see how he reacts, then you can worry about everything else."

Happy about it? That seemed doubtful. It would be nice, but I just couldn't see it happening.

"I don't know..." I repeated. I shifted in my seat again. The whole thing was stressing me out.

"That's right. You don't know. But you're going to find out."

Tamara smiled at me and picked up the spoon off the table. She handed it to me. I smiled through my tears and pulled the pint of ice cream closer.

"Thank you for being the greatest best friend in the world," I said, squeezing her hand. "I don't think I'd be able to do this without you."

"Anytime, champ. Now, eat up. You have a big day ahead of you."

CHAPTER 20

LUKE

My workday was dragging by. I had no focus. Everything felt miserable. Hallie was still ignoring me. It was eating me alive that I didn't have any answers.

All I could think about was getting home and talking to Hallie. All the possibilities kept coming into my mind. And most of them just felt shitty.

I couldn't decide whether I was dreading or anticipating our conversation. I had the worst feeling she would come over to tell me the baby was someone else's. She'd end up breaking it off with me and I'd lose everything with her.

The idea was enough to make me feel sick. But all I could do was trudge through my day. I would know for sure soon enough.

After what seemed like an eternity, my shift ended. I headed home and hopped into the shower.

As soon as I was out, I heard the doorbell. I was so anxious to talk to her that I answered the door in a towel.

Hallie's eyes snapped open when she saw my state. She

looked away quickly. I might have laughed if I wasn't so nervous.

It took me a moment to find my voice. I cleared my throat and stepped aside, holding the door open for her to enter.

"Hallie, it's good to see you. Come inside, please."

She nodded and I led her into the living room. We sat on the couch together in silence for a few moments. Finally, she sighed and looked at me.

"I'm sorry I've been avoiding you," she said. "I wasn't sure how to tell you what I need to say."

I nodded, though my chest tightened. It had been hellish, but she didn't need to know that. "I understand. But you don't owe me anything. We never really talked about being exclusive…"

The words stung as I spoke them, but I meant it. She didn't have to put herself on hold for me, even though I didn't have eyes for anyone but her.

"What do you mean?" she asked, looking genuinely confused for a moment. "Oh, wait. You think… no, Luke. I haven't been with anyone but you. The baby is yours."

It took me several moments to process what she told me. It didn't seem real.

All the agony and tension left my body. I felt a sense of elation and jumped up off the couch with a huge smile.

"It is? I'm really the father?"

Hallie stared at me. Her lips pulled into a soft smile. "Yeah, Luke. You're really the father. There hasn't been anyone else."

I grinned at her, and she glanced at my crotch.

"You lost your towel," she said. I looked down and realized I was standing there nude.

Grabbing the towel from the floor, I wrapped it around

my waist and returned to my seat on the couch. "Are you... having the baby?"

"Yes, I am." She nodded with certainty.

I ran a hand through my hair. "I can't believe it, Hallie. I'm going to be a dad..."

It was a possibility I had never dared to hope for, but all my life I'd randomly thought about things I'd want to teach my child. I just figured it would never happen because I never seemed to find the right woman.

I'd told myself I didn't want to have kids so I wouldn't feel sad about it. So I wouldn't mourn the life I'd never live.

Now, it was really happening. And I could do it with this woman who took my breath away every time I saw her.

"Yeah," Hallie said, looking away. "I'm going to have the baby, and you can be in its life if that's really what you want. It wouldn't be fair to either of you to keep that from you."

Wait. This wasn't what I had been hoping to hear. My heart began to sink. "Oh. Right."

Hallie seemed to sense that I wasn't happy about it because she sighed. She looked at me and spoke directly. Her tone was firm.

"Come on, Luke. You know we can't be in a relationship. We're clearly incompatible. We can co-parent, though. And the baby will get to have us both."

I let the information sink in, trying to hide my bitter disappointment. I hadn't realized how much I wanted a relationship with her until she had taken it off the table. Turns out, that was *exactly* what I wanted.

And she didn't, even though I could tell she was just as crazy about me as I was about her. But that didn't mean I had to give up the idea. There would be time enough to work this all out with her.

"Thank you for being honest with me," I said, smiling at her. I wouldn't let her know that I was hurt by the rejection.

She needed strength right now, and I was good at strength. "I'm glad that you live next door. That'll make it easy to be with you during appointments. I can drive you to every appointment and exam. I want to be there for all of it."

It was true, too. I wanted to be involved every step of the way. I would understand some of the medical side of things that Hallie wouldn't. She would be better off with me there.

All I wanted was to protect her. And protect my baby.

God, I couldn't believe that I was going to be a father. And I couldn't believe how happy the idea made me.

The only thing that would have made it better was if Hallie wanted to parent with me. I'd suddenly gotten the idea in my head of a real family.

And I wanted Hallie to be a part of that. It shocked me, but it was as clear as day. I wanted her.

Hallie stood from the couch without regarding what I had said. It made me feel another rush of disappointment. She really didn't want anything to do with me, did she?

It stung.

"I've got to go tell my parents."

I cringed. I could only imagine how that conversation was going to go. I didn't envy her for it.

"Of course. I'm here if you need anything."

She nodded without meeting my eye. "Thanks, Luke."

"Anytime. Seriously. I'm always right here or a phone call away. Remember that." I walked her to the door.

"Bye," she muttered. I tried to catch her eye, but she still wouldn't look at me.

"Bye."

I watched her as she took off through my yard and crossed into her own.

Hallie. Mother of my child. I kind of liked the sound of that.

I just wished that she did too.

CHAPTER 21

HALLIE

If I thought telling Luke was hard, it didn't even compare to the anxiety of knowing that I had to tell my parents.

It was hard enough for them to think I was having sex. I could only imagine how they were going to react to me being pregnant.

"Mom, Dad," I called once I stepped through the front door. "Can I talk to you both for a few minutes?"

I already knew it wasn't going to be a short conversation, but I could hope. Most people got nervous butterflies during these situations, but right now, mine had morphed into bats. I paced through the living room, completely on edge until they both came to greet me.

"Hallie, is everything okay?" my mother asked.

I didn't even know how to respond.

"I think we need to sit down for this," I said.

I sat in an armchair, and they took the couch. Once we were all settled, I placed my hand on my abdomen. It was a soothing habit I'd adopted since I found out the news.

My baby. A little living person who was sharing a body

with me right that moment. I'd never feel alone in the world again.

"What's going on, Hallie?" my dad asked. His tone was serious, as if he wanted to take control of the conversation.

I could already tell the direction this would go, and I dreaded it.

"I have some news," I said, finding the courage to meet his eyes, then my mother's. "And it's pretty big."

"All right," she said. "Just tell us. It'll be okay, whatever it is."

I closed my eyes, trying not to cry. "I'm pregnant."

The room was so silent I could have heard a pin drop.

Finally, my mom took in a sharp breath of air. "Out of wedlock?" she whispered.

I tried not to roll my eyes right in front of her and fortunately succeeded. "Yes."

If my annoyance was enough to make the lump in my throat go away, I would have been a much happier woman. Unfortunately, I tried to swallow it and felt a tear roll down my cheek.

"Hallie, is this some sort of prank?" my father demanded. "You know how I feel about pranks."

I sighed and wiped my eyes. It was probably the last thing in the world he had been expecting to hear.

"It's not a prank, Dad. I'm pregnant."

"Hallie, how could this have happened?" my mother exclaimed.

"Sex?" I offered, then instantly considered it the world's worst joke of all time.

My mother looked mortified. It almost made me feel better. "Hallie, please!"

"Don't use that language in front of your mother!"

I sighed and leaned back in my seat. "I'm sorry."

"Well, who got you pregnant? We need to have a talk with

him," Mom said. "There is a lot of planning to do. I assume you're going to—"

"I'd rather you didn't get involved with all of that," I said quickly. The idea of admitting to them that it was Luke was terrifying. I didn't want them to think less of him for some reason.

"Who's the father, Hallie?" Dad demanded.

I took a deep breath. They were going to find out eventually.

"Luke Beckett."

"God have mercy," my mother muttered, pinching the bridge of her nose.

"*Dr.* Beckett? From next door?" Dad asked, confused.

"Yes."

Dad curled his hands into fists. "The nerve of that guy. Who does he think he is, messing around with some girl half his age?" He rose to his feet. "I ought to go have a word with him."

Mom put a hand on his shoulder to calm him down. "Sit down, Chuck. No sense losing your head."

He sat back down, but he was still fuming. Silence stretched out in the room.

Finally, my mom said with a huff, "At least he's a doctor."

"Exactly. He's a *doctor*. He's so much older than you, Hallie!" Dad said. His face was red.

"And he's been a bachelor for who knows how long. It's a little late in life for him. If he hasn't settled down yet, he's the type who never will," she said.

My dad shook his head. "I can't believe this. After everything we've done for you."

That hurt. I never wanted them to be ashamed of me.

"He's not the right man for you, Hallie. How old is he, forty?"

"Thirty-seven," I muttered. Dad scoffed.

"This is why you should have found a man to marry before you went around..." My mother lowered her voice. "Having *sex* with him! I'd hoped you would wait until your wedding day. But you march to your own drum and always have."

I blinked, unsure of whether my mom was intentionally calling me a slut or if I was just having pregnancy hormones. I decided it wasn't important and tried my best to stay on track with the conversation.

"Look. I already know that he's not a good match for me," I said. "I told him that we could co-parent the baby without being in a relationship."

"*Co-parent?*" my mother exclaimed. "Honey, a child needs a family. A *real* family. Co-parenting is a last resort. Not something for a new mother!"

I groaned. It seemed like even when we were on the same page, my parents would never be able to see eye to eye with me.

"I will give my baby a real family. It'll have a mom and a dad and grandparents. You know that."

"It's not the same," my mother insisted. I felt a slight stabbing in my chest. I knew she was right, but it wasn't their choice. It was better this way.

It had to be.

"It doesn't have to be the same," I said, only half believing my own words. "We can still love one another. That's what being a family is supposed to be about. Not just what tradition dictates."

"A home is about stability, Hallie," my father said firmly. "A child needs stability more than anything. You think he'll be happy hopping from house to house every weekend?"

"Did Luke say he didn't want to marry you, honey? Is that what this is really about?"

"*What?*" It took all I had not to be affected by my mom's

ridiculous statement. "No, Mom. It was my choice. Luke and I don't get along well. It would be worse to raise a child in a home where their parents are always fighting."

She blinked. "So he *wanted* to marry you, and you said no?"

I groaned. "No. He didn't say anything about marriage. But he did seem to be interested in getting more seriously involved with me. I already know it's a bad idea."

"But *why?*" she asked.

"For all the reasons you guys already mentioned! He's older than me. He's not the guy for me. We're just not compatible."

Maybe if I kept listing all the reasons, I could convince myself I was making the right choice. I couldn't help but be drawn to Luke, but that didn't mean that we were good for each other. In fact, he pissed me off constantly.

My father nodded. In a sense, he seemed to accept the idea of co-parenting more than my mother did. Still, he was clearly not impressed with the situation.

"You never look before you leap, do you, Hal?" he asked, standing up. He looked at my mother expectantly, and she stood as well. "This conversation is over."

They left the room. I felt like I'd been slapped in the face.

The next few days were just as bad.

I couldn't be in the same room with my parents for longer than three minutes without a lecture or a dirty look from one of them. We were fighting constantly.

If there was one thing I had always known about pregnant women, it was that they were supposed to avoid stress. And I felt like a frog in boiling water.

The morning of the third day, I couldn't take any more. I

told Mom that it was flawed for her to think that marriage was right for every family.

She got up from the table and took the breakfast she'd made me away without a word.

That was the last straw. I got up from the table and stormed out of the house. I went directly to Luke's house and knocked furiously at the door. I didn't even know if he was home or not.

I was flooded with relief when the door opened. "Hallie?"

I was grateful that he hadn't answered the door in a towel this time. Maybe a little disappointed, too, but that didn't matter.

"Can I come in?" I asked, feeling suddenly awkward.

I had kind of brushed him off the last time we'd spoken. I wouldn't have blamed him if he decided to slam the door in my face.

He smiled at me instead, capturing me in those beautiful blue eyes of his. "Of course. Come on in. Are you okay?"

I stepped inside and he led me to his kitchen. It smelled heavenly in there and he pulled a chair out at the table. I sat down, trying to figure out what to say. "Not really."

He was already at his cabinet, taking out a plate and glass. He set them in front of me before he began to serve the food he'd prepared. Scrambled eggs. Toast. Bacon and sausage. Wholesome and hearty.

"What's going on?" he asked, catching me in his gaze again.

He looked concerned. Was that genuine, or did I just want to see it? I couldn't afford to be delusional with him.

"My parents have been giving me a really hard time about everything. I almost wish I hadn't told them."

Luke sighed with an understanding nod. He collected silverware from a drawer and gave it to me, then sat down across from me at the table. "I'm really sorry to hear that."

I sighed. "They're acting like I did the most horrible thing on earth. My dad will barely look at me, and if he does, it's with such malice or disappointment. And my mom is constantly lecturing me and trying to make me feel bad about getting pregnant out of wedlock."

Luke let out a low breath. "That's rough."

I nodded. "They're completely intolerant of anything I try to say or do. And my mom got all petty and took my breakfast away because we were fighting. So I came over here."

"You must have smelled my famous scrambled eggs. It gets them every time."

I rolled my eyes but couldn't help but smile. "I must have. Thank you, by the way. You didn't have to feed me."

Luke looked at me, his handsome face serious. "I wanted to. You're eating for two, remember? And one of those two happens to be my child."

My reluctant smile turned into something much warmer. But I couldn't get lost in this. It would be the biggest mistake I'd ever made if I did.

"Still. Thank you."

Luke was quiet for a moment as we ate, and then he looked at me again. "You shouldn't be living like that, you know. It's toxic. It could hurt you and the baby."

I sighed. "I know. I was thinking about that today."

"Would you think I'm absolutely crazy if I proposed something?"

I looked at him curiously. "I can't answer that honestly until you propose it."

Luke chuckled. "Move in with me. Here."

I blinked at Luke, caught entirely off guard. "Here?"

He nodded. "I have a spare room. And it's quiet. I work all the time. And you wouldn't have to put up with your parents' bullshit."

CRYSTAL MONROE

I sighed and rubbed my face. While it was tempting, it was also a terrifying idea.

"We would kill each other."

"You don't know that. We're not killing each other right now, are we?"

"No, but that might only be because you're feeding me."

Luke laughed. "You would have as much space to yourself as you could possibly want. I would give you whatever you needed. I just want to take care of you, Hallie."

I was lost in his eyes for another long moment. I could feel the sincerity in them. He really wanted this.

And I was surprised to realize that I did too. Shocked, even.

"Are you sure about that, Luke? It's a huge thing to offer. You might regret it."

"I won't," he said. He was burning with conviction. It was so hard to believe that he would put himself out like this for me.

"If we do this… I think it's best that our relationship stays platonic," I said. "I don't think we should try to be intimate or romantic. Everything is already complicated enough without adding all that into it."

I sighed, hating the way it felt to say this. "I won't be staying in your room with you. I'd want to be in the guest bedroom."

Luke was quiet for a moment, but he nodded. "Agreed. Whatever you want. As long as you're out of that stressful house. I want to keep you and the baby safe, and this seems like the best way I can do it right now."

I smiled at him. "Thank you."

He grinned at me, and I had to kick myself for the way it made my heart flip-flop.

Luke worked fast. He insisted that I move in right away.

After breakfast, I went back home to prepare for the

move. It seemed crazy and sudden, but the truth was, I was more than ready for a change.

My parents were less than thrilled about it. But since they were so disappointed in me, what was one more thing?

The next day, Luke and I waited until they were at the hardware store working. He helped me move all my things into his house. Actually, he did most of the moving. He insisted I stay off my feet, which I thought was ridiculous. So I mostly showed him what I wanted.

When we were finished and he set down the last box, he looked over at me and smiled.

"Welcome home."

Why I liked the sound of that so much was beyond me. Still, this was purely platonic, and I had to ignore all these irrational feelings. It was probably just hormones.

What I did know for sure was that I was relieved not to be living under my parents' roof anymore. It had been way too stressful. In fact, I decided to unwind with a long bath.

"Thanks, Luke."

"You hungry? I have some steaks I could cook for dinner."

"Nah, I'm not really hungry right now. Is it okay if I take a bath?"

"Of course. This is your home, too, now. Make yourself comfortable."

"Thanks." I smiled and went to my room.

Maybe we could pull off this platonic thing. Maybe he wouldn't be so annoying if we weren't sleeping together.

I could do this. I could live here, at least for a while until I figured things out.

And I could raise my baby with Luke's help.

I dug through my bags to gather what I would need and ducked into the guest bathroom to fill the bathtub. Once I was relaxing in the warm, soapy bubbles, I sighed with relief.

It was good to get away from my parents. I was already beginning to feel the stress melting away.

I loved them, but I'd never had a moment's peace since I moved back in with them. I just wasn't going to be the perfect daughter they wanted.

I gazed down at my abdomen. Resting my hand against it, I began to hum and sing to my baby.

It might have been a bit silly, but I felt connected to my little one. Somehow, having space away from my parents helped me to think a little more clearly.

When I was finished, I wrapped a towel around my body and began to walk to my room. I paused when I passed Luke's bedroom. I noticed that the door was cracked open.

I couldn't resist and peeked inside. I couldn't help but gape at what I saw. He was standing in his room topless, his broad chest bared.

My eyes roamed his muscled torso involuntarily. There was nothing I could do to stop myself. He was just so gorgeous.

It took all I had not to push the door open and step inside. My body burned for him, but my brain was telling me to stop. It just wasn't a good idea, no matter how good it would feel.

I forced myself to look away. I had to retreat into my bedroom to hide. If I didn't, I would make a massive mistake.

If we started sleeping together again, it would inevitably cause us to start fighting. It was more important than ever that I maintain the boundaries that I had set.

The last thing I needed would be to live in another environment where I couldn't get along with my housemates. I needed this to work out. Not just for me, but for our baby.

But when I was lying in bed, all I could think about was how much I wanted to go back to Luke's room. I let out a heavy sigh. This was going to be harder than I thought.

CHAPTER 22

LUKE

I smiled at the redheaded woman who had been with Hallie on the first day I'd met her. Tamara, an ultrasound technician at Lakeview Hospital, was sitting at Hallie's side.

They were both beaming at the screen that would soon show our baby.

It had been a bit over a month since Hallie had moved in, and it was her first ultrasound. To say I was nervous and excited would be an understatement.

"Everything is ready now," Tamara informed us.

My attention snapped to the screen. My chest was tight, which surprised me. I didn't really understand why I would have such a visceral reaction to something like this. Then again, I had never been a father before.

The screen lit up and a soft thudding sound filled the room. The heartbeat.

"Everything sounds good." Tamara squinted at the screen and sucked in air. "Oh, my goodness, Hal. Can you hear that?"

"What?" Hallie asked tightly.

"There are *two* heartbeats. And look, you can see them both here," Tamara said, gesturing to the screen, though I was already seeing it all for myself.

"That means..." Hallie broke off.

"Twins!" Tamara exclaimed.

I couldn't look away from the screen until I heard Hallie gasp. I met her eyes, and I swear there was an electricity between us. An ESP shared thought.

What?

Tamara squealed. "I'm going to be a double aunt! Not bad for my first time."

I was glad she was there to lighten the mood, because I was too stunned to speak. Twins. We were going to have *two* children.

Wow.

Hallie looked over at the screen, her eyes filled with tears. "Why didn't I know there were two of them?" she said, her voice low but amused. I smiled over at her, and to my surprise, she smiled back.

"Well, sometimes it can be quite a shock!" Tamara chuckled and allowed us to gaze at the tiny forms. "Don't be too hard on yourself."

"I can't believe it," I murmured. Hallie laughed.

"It's crazy, right? I wonder how my parents will react when they find out I'm not having just one, but *two* babies out of wedlock."

Tamara snorted. "They're going to be thrilled, especially once the babies get here. Right now, it's all just hard for them to digest. Those two are really set in their ways."

"Tell me about it," Hallie said.

"Don't worry about that right now," I said. "Look at our babies."

The truth was, I didn't want Hallie to be stressing herself out about her family any more than she already had. She was alone with me now for a reason. And this was too special a moment to let her parents ruin it.

"They're beautiful, aren't they?"

I smiled. Truth was, they were just little peanuts and sort of hard to distinguish from everything else in the gray mass in the ultrasound. But they really were the most beautiful little peanuts.

"They are."

I couldn't keep the huge smile from spreading across my face. I couldn't wait to meet them.

The rest of the appointment went well. On the way back home, Hallie looked over at me, her eyes round. I already knew what that meant.

"Chicken?"

She nodded sheepishly, and I couldn't help but smile. Spicy roasted chicken with rosemary potatoes had been her biggest pregnancy craving so far. I had the kitchen well stocked to accommodate her.

I set to work cooking as soon as we got back. Hallie went upstairs to bathe, and by the time she was done, dinner was on the table. She came down looking fresh and rejuvenated.

"I followed my nose," she said with a little laugh.

I felt a stab of unease at just how adorable I found it. She was so beautiful. But she wanted us to just be friends and co-parents.

"Dinner is served!" I said, sitting down to our meal. "Just like the doctor ordered."

"Dr. Luke knows what he's talking about," Hallie said with a big smile. She was already digging into her meal, and I chuckled before I began eating my own.

"Twins, Luke. Isn't that wild?" she said, looking up at me with sparkling eyes. "It's going to be so much work."

I grinned. "I'm up for the challenge if you are," I said.

"Oh, I'm so up for it!"

"I wonder if they will be identical," I said with a smile. "Or fraternal."

"And will they both be little boys? Little girls? A little girl and a little boy?" Hallie wiggled excitedly in her seat before bringing more chicken to her lips. "I can't wait to meet them, Luke."

"Me neither," I agreed with a smile.

"This is so good. It has been making the perfect writing fuel, actually."

I looked up at Hallie curiously. "Writing fuel?"

She shifted again, this time looking a little bit shy. But then she fixed a bright smile on me. "Actually, yeah. I've been working on a book, and I just finished it."

I paused with my fork in the air and stared at her.

A book? This was news to me. That meant I'd had a lot of things wrong for a very long time.

"You wrote a *book*?"

"Uh-huh."

"Hallie, that's incredible," I said. "Congratulations! What kind of a book is it? What's it about?"

She blushed and looked down at her plate. Modest, too. No wonder she had never told me about it before.

"Well, it's a romance book. It's about a couple who have a hard time getting along, but ultimately can't resist one another."

I felt my lips twitch but didn't allow myself to smile despite how adorable I found it that she had probably modeled her couple after us. Or maybe not. But either way, I couldn't deny the similarities.

Not that we had a happy ending in our romantic future by any means. Still, it was a nice thought. I liked the idea of maybe influencing something as impressive as a book.

"That's amazing," I said. "I can't believe you've been

working on something like that all this time and didn't tell me."

Hallie chuckled. "I didn't want you to make fun of me. And thank you for not."

"Why would I make fun of you for having the ambition and passion to do something so big? I'm not sure why you didn't just tell me to shut my damn mouth."

"I didn't think you would listen." Hallie quirked her brow, and I couldn't help but laugh.

"I can see why."

"So now you know the truth. I wrote a book."

"I do."

"Do you read?"

I laughed. "Do you mean *can* I read?"

This dissolved her into giggles. When she recovered herself, she shook her head. "What I'm trying to ask is do you *want* to read my book?"

I grinned. "I would love to read it, Hallie."

"Awesome!"

After we'd finished our dinner and cleaned up, Hallie went up to her room and came back down to deliver a copy of her book to me. I took the stack of papers, impressed with just how much work had clearly gone into it.

"You've been busy," I said.

She blushed again. "It's a little long, but hopefully it doesn't drag."

"It's a book; it's supposed to be long. I just haven't ever seen a manuscript like this before."

"I'm old fashioned. I could have emailed a digital copy to you, but there's something special about reading words right off the paper. I had a few copies made."

"I love it," I said, flipping through the pages. "I have to warn you, though. I'm not familiar with the romance genre.

Most of my reading has been nonfiction. But I can't wait to read this."

Hallie smiled. "Okay. Take your time with it. And let me know what you think when you're done! Even if you don't like it."

I raised a brow at Hallie. "You think I'd hold back my constructive criticism?"

"Fair point." She laughed, then stood and yawned. "I'm headed to bed. Good night, Luke."

"Good night, Hallie."

I watched her as she went upstairs, then began my own bedtime routine. Once I got into bed, I took the manuscript with me and began to read.

To my surprise, I couldn't put it down.

I was drawn into the story immediately. I completely forgot that she had a similar dynamic between the characters as we had in real life. I was so immersed in the story and characters that it was like a whole different world.

I stayed up all night reading. I didn't even realize how late it was until I saw the sun beginning to stream through my windows. I finally set the book down and tried to get a nap in.

I would have a very hungry pregnant woman to feed soon.

∽

I dragged myself out of bed and went downstairs to make myself some coffee. I usually avoided it but kept it on hand for when it was needed.

After it brewed, I sank down into one of the kitchen chairs to enjoy it. To my surprise, I heard Hallie enter the kitchen.

When I turned around to greet her, I was stunned for a

moment. She was wearing a tiny, almost sheer nightgown, and she looked more beautiful than I had ever seen her.

"Good morning, Luke."

I had to snap out of it. "Good morning, Hallie. I started to read your book."

Her already glowing face brightened. "Oh, really? What did you think?"

I grinned. "It's fantastic! I love it. All the characters are so realistic. I literally couldn't put it down. You're so talented."

She looked absolutely stunned to hear my words. All it did was encourage me to say more about what I had been thinking. "I think that you should submit it to an agent."

"An agent?"

I nodded. "It's the best way to get it published."

"You think I could be published?" Her voice was soft and surprised.

"I know you could be published," I corrected. "If you do it right. You could submit it to some places directly, but for the best chance of success, you can do it through an agent. If you have good representation, you can get a good contract."

Hallie stood there as if I had said something entirely impossible for her to comprehend. She looked away for a moment. I let my eyes roam her body.

My attention shifted to her breasts. Her nipples looked a bit swollen. I wasn't sure, but it looked almost as if her breasts were already growing. Was that even possible?

She looked too good to resist. When she looked back at me, there was fire in my gaze. Her face darkened in a flush, and without thinking or being able to help myself, I pulled her onto my lap.

She sighed in pleasure as my hard cock made contact with her perfect round ass. I rubbed it against her, and she let out a soft moan. I had never known a woman I wanted so much.

I felt her body respond to my advances and had the overpowering urge to taste her. I stood, holding her carefully and sitting her in my place. I knelt in front of her and gently parted her legs.

She gasped softly as I ran my hands up and down her thighs, slowly sliding her nightie up. "Do you want me to stop?" I murmured, bringing my mouth to her left thigh for a light kiss.

She moaned and shook her head, putting her hands in my hair. I tugged her panties down and let them fall to the floor. I pressed my mouth into her heat, pleased by the hiss of enjoyment I heard from her.

When I tasted her, I let out a low moan of appreciation. She tasted amazing. I was shocked when it took just a few tongue strokes of her clit to feel her quake.

Her breath grew heavy as I began to try to prolong her orgasm, but it didn't make a difference. Instead, I decided to meet the speed of its pace. It enhanced her pleasure, and I could feel her climax against my tongue.

"Come on," I said, standing up and offering Hallie my hand. She took it and I led her to my bedroom.

We made it to my bed and I climbed on top of her, pressing a tender kiss against her neck as I took my time undressing us both. She squirmed beneath me, her face flushed. Her hands roamed my body, and I felt an urgent pressure in my abdomen.

I wanted her *now*.

Once we were undressed, I slid my cock along her slit and felt her arch against me. I had a brief concern about the babies, but I knew that it was still safe to have sex. And on the plus side, I didn't need a condom this time.

She was already knocked up.

Hallie bucked her hips against me, seeming more needy than I had ever seen her before. I was ready to meet that energy and began to slide myself inside her. I couldn't help but moan.

She felt so good. And I had wanted her for so long. Hallie gasped once I had my full length inside her, and I froze.

"Are you okay?"

She smiled at me, and I still didn't relax. "Yeah. It just feels *really* good. Like. Extra good. I missed you."

I chuckled and nodded. "Okay. Good. I missed you too."

I leaned down and pressed a soft kiss against her lips. She returned it before I began to thrust into her in earnest.

Hallie's hands clutched my back as I felt her respond to me. My abdomen was burning with need. It was hard to hold myself back, but I maintained a steady motion.

When she cried out and I felt her pussy clenching around me, I couldn't restrain myself. I buried myself deep inside her. I thrust urgently and felt the strength of her climax soaring through my veins.

I wasn't ready to come yet, so I pulled out of her and allowed her sensitivities to cool down. I continued to rub myself against her, however. I was surprised when I felt her hands grip my waist.

She tugged me closer, implying that she wanted me back. I was relieved since I hadn't been able to reach my own climax yet. I plunged into her, sensing the intensity of her desire.

She let out a cry of rapture as I began to fuck her in earnest. I realized it had been exactly what she wanted. She writhed beneath me like an animal in heat. I almost came right there and then.

My hands roamed all over her beautiful body. The way it was changing and growing was so attractive to me. I couldn't get enough of it.

I felt her body tense beneath me and dropped my mouth around one of her perky, swollen nipples. She moaned and arched her back. As my tongue enhanced her pleasure, I began to pick up my pace until I knew I wouldn't be able to stop myself anymore.

Fortunately, she let out a telling moan and her body shuddered beneath me. I felt the heat of my own orgasm begin searing through me. Hallie trembled and I felt her release surrounding me. Her walls began to milk my cock, and I pumped her full of my cum.

I pulled out gently and rolled over onto the opposite side of her. Not even thinking, I scooped her into my arms and pressed a kiss against the top of her head.

And, because I had been up all night reading her book, I fell asleep almost immediately.

CHAPTER 23

HALLIE

If anyone would have told me that pregnancy would make my sex drive surge the way it did, I might have thought twice about living with Luke.

But nobody did. And as much as I hadn't wanted to fall into the trap of a sexual relationship with him, I hadn't been able to help myself. In fact, it had become a nightly ritual for us to have sex.

And it was really, *really* good sex, too.

Then again, that wasn't surprising. Luke and I had always had amazing sexual chemistry. And with the changes that were happening in my body, I wanted him more than I ever had before. It felt amazing.

"Move into my bedroom," Luke said one morning over breakfast. I looked up at him in surprise.

"What?"

"I think you should move into my bedroom. You have a hard time sleeping alone in the guest room, and you and the babies need good rest. Besides, I really like having you in there with me."

I sat at the table in silence for a moment. Was it really a

good idea? To be honest, it did feel inevitable. It hadn't been what I wanted to happen at first, but things weren't what I'd expected.

In fact, I had been surprised by the way he had been supporting me. He hadn't even been pushing me to go to grad school or making fun of my lack of career ambition. After he had read my book, he'd been taking me a lot more seriously.

"I guess we can try it," I said. "If you're sure you're okay with that."

"I wouldn't be saying it if I wasn't sure, Hallie."

Luke caught me in his bright-blue eyes and smiled. Why was he so damn handsome?

"Okay."

"Perfect. I'll start helping you move things in when we're done eating."

I smiled and scarfed down my food, wondering what this meant for our relationship. We hadn't put any labels on it or anything, but things had been going really well. Better than I could have hoped for.

And no matter what the label of our relationship might be, I knew he would be an incredible father to our children. I was happy with where our relationship had gone.

Our twins were going to be so lucky.

We cohabited comfortably for several weeks. To my surprise, I couldn't have been happier. I felt like we were really on the same page about everything.

One night, Luke had worked late, so I decided to surprise him and make him dinner, wearing nothing but an apron. I was hoping that when he saw me greet him that way, he wouldn't be able to resist. He enjoyed our sexual relationship just as much as I did.

I wasn't disappointed. When I heard him begin to unlock the door, I opened it before he was able to finish. His eyes bulged, and I smiled.

"Come have dinner," I said. "I made your favorite."

"You're my favorite," he said in a low growl, reaching for me. I grinned and stepped out of reach.

"No touching. It's time to eat."

He let out a low hum and then nodded. "Interesting. Okay."

"Come on."

He raised a brow but allowed it. I pointed him to his seat, and he complied with a smile. "It smells good. I didn't realize you knew what my favorite meal is."

"I pay attention," I said with a wink.

"I can smell that."

I chuckled and got his plate ready, then set it down in front of him. He tried to reach for me again and I used the spatula I was holding to gently bump his hand away. "No touching, remember?"

He didn't seem pleased with this, but still smiled. "You know, it's going to be hard for me to eat with you looking like that."

"Well then, you'd better start because the longer the food is on your plate, the longer it will be before you can touch me."

He sighed dramatically and began to cut into his steak. He smiled when he saw the inside of it. "Perfect medium rare. Thank you, Hallie."

"You're welcome," I said, taking my place across from him at the table. He continued cutting and took a bite.

"This is delicious, but you know, as a doctor I have to

inform you that this is making me want to rush to eat. And rushing to eat is not ideal for the digestive system."

"Then you're just going to have to take your time, aren't you?"

His gaze was smoldering, but he nodded and took another bite. "I guess I will."

He did manage to eat his dinner, but the second he was finished, he wiped his mouth with his napkin and stood.

"I want you," he demanded.

He chased me through the house, and we tumbled into bed. I let out a pleased moan as he unleashed his hard cock from his pants and pressed it against me. He felt so good, and I had wanted him all day.

He thrust inside me, going gently at first, and then ultimately picking up speed. He brought me quickly to my climax and unleashed his own inside me.

I yawned and closed my eyes. He had been right when he said I slept better in his bed, because soon I was drifting off.

I jumped when Luke spoke, startling me back to my fully awake state.

"Have you sent your book to an agent yet, Hallie?"

I looked over at Luke and smiled. "Not yet. I haven't found the time."

He sighed and pulled away from me, settling on the other side of the bed. "Really? Seems to me like you have nothing but time being here."

"There's no rush on that," I pointed out. "There's plenty of time."

"Come on, Hallie. You should have been starting this process as soon as you began writing the book! It's really not that hard. You really need to have some direction in life. You're going to be a mother, for Chrissake."

I felt pain panging in my chest and turned away from him. I wanted to hide the prickling tears in my eyes. How was it that we had suddenly just reverted to everything about our relationship that I hated?

"Exactly, Luke. I'm going to be a mother. Maybe I have other things on my mind than just trying to find an agent."

"Like making dinner in the nude? I'm sure that took as much time as mailing a manuscript would."

That one stung.

"It's not just a manuscript, Luke. I have to write a query letter and research the agents too. They like these things to be personal or they will dismiss them."

"Sounds like more excuses to blow around in the wind to me," Luke said. "Come on, Hal. You can do this. Have a little confidence in yourself."

I didn't even reply to him. I was too choked up and I didn't feel like fighting. Instead, I grew quiet and pretended that I had fallen asleep.

I was crushed. If Luke was always going to be this critical, did I even really want to be in a relationship with him? He thought that I lacked direction, but if anything, being pregnant had given me more than I had ever had before.

I already knew that I cared deeply for Luke. In fact, I'd never been happier in thinking about the two of us being real parents, in a real family. He would be an incredible father.

I knew what kind of life I wanted to have. I knew what kind of mother I wanted to be, and I wanted to live life on my own terms.

But would Luke ever let me do that in peace?

CHAPTER 24

LUKE

I woke up to my alarm and sat up, stretching. It was going to be a good day. I glanced over to Hallie, who was still sleeping.

"Hal," I said, rustling her shoulder. I liked to greet her before I went to work because some days were long and grueling.

She made a soft, sleepy sound and turned to face me. "Hmm?"

I smiled at her, my heart full. She was so beautiful. "Good morning."

"Morning."

"I'm going to get ready for work now." Then, remembering our conversation from the night before, I teased her. "You better have an agent by the end of the day. I don't want the mother of my children being lazy."

I figured it might be nice for her to start the day with a little bit of encouragement. I knew it could be hard for her to get focused. I was happy to help.

I pressed a kiss on top of her head and headed to the

shower. I had no doubt Hallie could make something of her writing talent. She just needed a little motivation.

When I got to work, I ran into Ryder in the hallway. I'd seen him a few times outside of work the past few weeks. He and a few of the other doctors were becoming good friends of mine.

"Hey, Luke! How's Hallie?"

I warmed with pride. "She's doing really well. We're both excited and counting down the weeks till we're parents."

Ryder chuckled. "There's nothing quite like it."

"I can imagine. Man… I can't believe I'm having twins."

Ryder's laughter came easily. "It's going to be quite an experience. It can be a bit challenging even with one, but if the two of you are on the same page, you should be able to tackle the parenting thing with no problem."

I smiled. "I think that Hallie and I make a great team. In fact, she might even end up making more money than me one day. I just have to give her a little bit of encouragement sometimes. I think she doubts herself too much."

"Oh, yeah? It's great that you two can be there to support each other. I think that you're going to have such a good time being parents. It's so much fun."

I smiled. I'd been thinking more and more about what it would be like to have our little family. Every day that passed was a day that brought our children closer to being born. I was over the moon about it.

It didn't even matter what gender the babies were. I would do everything with them. I'd play sports, take them fishing, build things with them. I'd do anything that made them happy.

"I'm really excited about it. I have big plans for us. I already can't wait for them to walk and talk."

Ryder laughed heartily. "Might want to slow down a bit,

my friend. It's going to go much faster than you think. I'd say it's a good idea to just try to enjoy each moment as it comes."

I chuckled. "I guess I am getting a little ahead of myself. I'm just really excited to be a dad, man."

"Trust me, I get it," Ryder said with a laugh. "It's going to be an amazing experience for you both. You're a lucky guy."

I smiled and we chatted a little longer before I had to head in to work.

The ER was busy, but luckily, we didn't have any patients that were severe today. Still, it was a long day, and I was excited to get back home to see Hallie.

I parked my car in the garage and headed inside. Maybe she would tell me she had sent her book out to an agent.

"Honey, I'm home," I called lightheartedly when I walked through the door.

I was surprised when I was met with silence. Usually, she greeted me at the door. I felt a spike of panic. "Hal, are you okay?"

When again, there was no answer, I tore through the house looking for her. She wasn't in the living room or any other room, and I ran my hand through my hair in a panic. When I checked my bedroom, I was surprised to find a note.

Dear Luke,

This is really hard for me to write, but it has to be said. I don't appreciate the way you keep trying to control my life. I don't need you telling me how to live it, as it's mine and only mine. You're still welcome to be a dad to the babies, but I think that it's best that we separate. I've already packed my things and I will be staying back at my parents' house. They may try to control things too, but it's because they're my parents. I shouldn't have to take it from a partner.

Hallie

I stared at the note, completely dumbfounded. When I looked around my bedroom, I saw that all her things had

DOCTOR'S SECRET TWINS

already been removed. There was nothing left of her here except the paper I clutched in my hands. The note that shattered my heart into a million pieces.

No. I couldn't allow this. I had been joking that morning. Hallie just didn't realize it.

All I had to do was go over to her parents' house and explain. Then we could get over the little misunderstanding and pretend it had never happened.

I let the note drop from my hands and hurried over to the Jones' house. My chest was so tight that I felt like I couldn't breathe.

I knocked on the door, probably a little too frantically. I was almost afraid that no one would answer and I would be cut off from Hallie entirely. Fortunately, the door swung open.

"Good evening, Mrs. Jones," I said, trying to conceal how disappointed I was that it hadn't been Hallie who had answered the door. "I really need to talk to Hallie. Could you get her for me, please?"

Mrs. Jones gave me a look that bordered between cold and sympathetic. "I'm sorry, Dr. Beckett, but Hallie isn't receiving visitors right now."

I wanted to plead to be allowed inside, but before I could think of the right thing to say, the door closed in my face.

I didn't wait to go home before I pulled my phone out to text her. I let her know I was outside and that I needed to talk. When she replied, I felt the pain in my chest grow even sharper.

Hallie: I don't feel like talking to you.

Luke: Come on, Hallie. I was joking this morning. I'm sorry if it upset you. We can work this out.

It took a few minutes before Hallie's response arrived. I didn't budge.

Hallie: Some jokes aren't funny, Luke. And there's truth in every joke. You keep acting like you have the right to control my life, but you don't. It's not okay.

I tried explaining myself, but she just wouldn't have it. She stopped replying entirely, so I went back to my house feeling totally rejected.

Everything had been so perfect between us. How could it come crashing down like this in the blink of an eye?

~

The next few days I had to work twelve-hour shifts. I didn't have many chances to reach out to Hallie, but in my down moments, I still tried.

Of course she wouldn't respond, so when I finally had a moment, I went over to her parents' house.

Mrs. Jones sighed when she opened the door.

"Hello again, Mrs. Jones. Could I please speak with Hallie?"

"I'm sorry, Luke, but she's out apartment hunting right now. Maybe when she comes back."

I felt a crushing weight at the news and managed to nod. "I see. Thank you."

Apartment hunting?

I went back to my house in a daze. She was going to find somewhere else to live. She was really serious about this.

Hallie wanted nothing to do with me.

Everything was falling apart.

When I got inside, I closed the door behind me and headed for the liquor cabinet. This was too much to bear without a stiff glass of whiskey.

CHAPTER 25

HALLIE

My heart was breaking. I missed being with Luke more than I ever thought I could. Why did he have to be such an asshole?

Even if it was true that he had been joking, it still wasn't okay. I wasn't going to let him control my life and criticize everything I did.

I had the strangest feeling that the babies were missing him too, but I couldn't be sure about that. Either way, I was. And I hated it.

I also hated the fact that my feet were swollen and sore because I had been working all day at the hardware store. I didn't have much of an option. I needed to make ends meet.

And it had become abundantly clear to me that I would never be able to live happily with my parents again. It was time to be independent.

I had told Luke I wanted to live my life on my own terms. Well, working at my parents' store was what I had to do to pull it off.

"Welcome, Ms. Jones," the landlord of the apartment building I was viewing said with a smile. "Right on time."

"Thank you. Hallie is fine."

"A pleasure. Let's take a look around the space, shall we?"

I nodded, though there was a knot in the pit of my stomach. While the apartment was nice enough, it didn't compare to the quality of life I had gotten used to in Luke's home. And it lacked the warmth of it entirely.

When the tour was concluded, the landlord turned to me with another big smile. "All right, what do you think? Not too bad for only twelve hundred a month."

I blinked. Had I heard him right? The tiny apartment cost that much every month?

"Um… it's really nice, yeah."

"Well, if you're interested, I would just need your first and last month's rent up front, plus a security deposit. The deposit will be returned to you if the apartment is in good shape when you leave."

I nodded dumbly as the landlord wrapped up, letting me know that I could let him know if I had any questions or was interested. I followed him outside and watched him leave in a shiny black car. Then I sat down on the steps and cried.

A thousand, two hundred dollars per month. And I'd have to give him so much just to move in, too. And the utilities weren't even included, either.

The whole thing just amplified the fact that I missed Luke. All I really wanted was to be back with him.

Every day with him until recently had been full of fun and possibilities. I could see us as a unit, the way we would raise our children together. I had been starting to feel like we could actually be a family.

I loved him, no matter how much it hurt to admit it. I just wished that he could be a little bit less of a jerk about things. It wasn't good for me to face that level of criticism, joking or not.

My heart was breaking tenfold. I couldn't be with Luke,

even though it was dawning on me just how deep my feelings for him were. We had never said we loved each other, but it didn't keep me from feeling it.

And now, I would never be able to afford the apartment on my wages, especially if I was taking care of twins. What was I going to do?

My phone rang suddenly, and I was sure it was going to be Luke again. Thankfully, it wasn't, because it hurt a little more every time I had to ignore his calls.

"Tamara, hi."

"You're crying. Why are you crying?"

For some reason the question just made me cry harder. Tamara was familiar with this about me by then and let me cry it out. Eventually I was able to speak again.

"I can't afford it!"

"Oh, Hal… is it really that much?"

She had known I would be looking at apartments today and had probably called to congratulate me. The realization made me cry again. These hormones were a pain.

"It's way too much. The only way I could do it is if I gave up writing and just worked my entire life away at the hardware store. God, maybe my parents were right…"

"Hal, calm down. You don't have to give up writing. Things are tough right now, but they always find a way to work out." Tamara sighed. "It's all going to be okay. I promise. And if nothing else, you and I can be roomies. It'll be fun. You'll want help with Double Trouble anyway."

I smiled to myself. Double Trouble was the nickname she had already given the twins. "I couldn't do that to you, Tamara."

"Oh, come on, like I'm doing amazing, groundbreaking things in the world to where I couldn't try to help out my best friend in her time of need."

The idea of a plan B did make me feel a little bit better,

but I knew I would never be able to take her up on it. It would be way too much to ask. Besides, she only had one bedroom where she lived. I'd be bunked up with the twins in the living room for who knew how long?

I needed to find a solution on my own. But either way, it was still a comforting thought and it cheered me up a little.

"Thanks, Tamara. It's not like I'll be homeless though. The worst-case scenario is I end up stuck with my parents. But I really feel like I have to get away from them. And I don't know how much longer I can stand being next door to Luke."

"Aww, sweetie…" Tamara's voice was gentle and sympathetic. "You're really having a hard time with all of this, huh?"

"I just want to be with him," I said, breaking down into tears again. "But it's not good for me to be with someone who doesn't understand me."

"I know. And it seemed like he was being a bit controlling. I can't believe he said it was a joke."

I sighed, thinking back on the conversation. He had been smiling and being sweet otherwise. So maybe he *had* been joking.

But it didn't change the conversation from the night before and how much it had stung. Then he had to rub it in like that the second I woke up. The whole thing just felt like shit, honestly.

"Bad joke, if it was. On a sensitive subject."

"Yeah…"

We were quiet for a moment. All I could think about was how much I wanted to be with Luke and how much it hurt that I just couldn't be. Everything could have been so perfect. But it was ruined.

"He really disappointed me, Tamara. I was really happy with him."

"I know," Tamara said soothingly. "But it's okay. There are plenty of other guys out there."

Not like Luke. And not for soon-to-be mothers who were apparently lazy failures.

"Yeah, but who is going to want to date someone with twins?"

"Plenty of guys. You're a great person, Hallie."

I didn't want to be cheered up, though. I wanted things to be right with Luke. I paused for a moment as I considered whether I should let Tamara know what I'd realized. Finally, I went for it.

"I think I love him. Isn't that stupid?"

"No... it's not stupid."

"Are you sure? Because it feels stupid to love someone so critical and judgmental."

"Well, you love him despite his flaws," Tamara pointed out. "You're asserting your boundaries. And that's really strong of you. And important. Even if it hurts like hell."

"Yeah," I said with a sniffle. "I guess you're right."

"You sound like you need some bestie time. Where are you at? I can come pick you up."

"I'm crying on the stoop of the apartment I will never have," I said with a laugh. "I can drive over to you."

"Are you okay to drive? You sound pretty upset."

I sniffed and took a deep breath. "Yeah. I'll have some water in the car and sit a minute before I go."

"If you're sure, Hal. Don't make me regret trusting you! Keep your eyes on the road and everything."

"I will."

"Two hands on the wheel! Check your mirrors!"

I laughed. "I *will*. Thank you."

"Anytime, bestie. See you and Double Trouble soon! Love you guys."

"I love you too."

It would be good to get out of my head for a little while and spend time with Tamara. Otherwise, I would just sit around all day because all I could think about was one thing.

I loved Luke, and I had lost him.

CHAPTER 26

LUKE

I dragged myself out of bed and showered quickly. I was going to be late for work if I didn't hurry, but I barely cared. Nothing felt like it mattered now that I'd lost Hallie.

I kicked an empty pizza box out of my way when I went into the kitchen. I was going to try a coffee, whether it made me late or not. My house was a pigsty these days.

I just hadn't had the motivation to clean, cook, or do much of anything. All I could do was be miserable. I'd lost Hallie.

Every idiotic dream that I'd had of having a perfect family with her was shattered. Every hope and dream had left me when she did. And now I felt like I had nothing left.

The worst part of it all was that I loved her.

I really and truly loved her. And I was an idiot and managed to mess up the whole thing. I don't know why I had even bothered to try.

That was the thing though. I hadn't tried to love her. It had just happened.

How could something so big and so intense just sneak up on a person? I had to be stupid not to have noticed.

Well, I obviously was stupid because I'd lost her.

I couldn't decide whether being right about that made me feel better or worse. Instead of trying to figure it out, I finished my coffee and headed to work.

I was only about ten minutes late, though compared to my typical punctuality, that was out of the ordinary. When I arrived, I clocked in, then made my way to my wing.

I waved half-heartedly at Ryder, Max, and Barrett. They were standing together at the nurses' station, talking.

"Hey, Luke," Ryder said. He frowned when he looked at me. "You're looking a bit rough today."

"Thanks. I didn't have time to shave."

The truth was, I hadn't had the motivation to shave. Or do much of anything else lately. I was in a deep depression.

"The salt-and-pepper look is good on you," Barrett teased. I snorted because I just didn't have the energy to laugh. I didn't really have the energy for any of this right now.

"No offense, guys, but I've got to go. I'm running late." I mustered a smile as genuine as I could make it, then headed to the ER.

It went by as slowly as it possibly could. I did my job well—I always had—but my passion was gone.

Instead of laughing and joking with patients, I simply left the room as soon as I was done with what I had to do. I could only offer half-hearted reassurances to them because it felt like my own emotional energy was in the negative.

I was so relieved by the time the end of my shift came. All I wanted was to go back home and sleep.

To my surprise, Ryder, Max, and Barrett were waiting for me outside. It almost felt like an ambush.

"You're coming out for some beers, man," Max said, slap-

DOCTOR'S SECRET TWINS

ping me on the back and guiding me to the parking lot. "I won't take no for an answer."

"I really don't feel like doing anything right now," I stated, thinking that this would be the end of the matter.

"Yeah, that's why you absolutely have to do it. We know you're having a hard time. It would do you some good to let loose a bit."

I tried to argue with the logic but couldn't. I supposed a little time with the guys couldn't hurt. It had been a while.

"Fine, but I'll have to leave early."

"You have tomorrow off," Ryder pointed out. "I already checked the schedule. We've been planning this little intervention for a while now."

I couldn't help but laugh. Leave it to these guys to really try and look out for me. I had no excuse now.

I nodded. "All right."

We made the journey to the bar and sat down at what had become our usual table. Truthfully, I hadn't been quite as inclined to join them once Hallie had moved in. I was always eager to get home and be with her.

Now all of that had changed. I didn't have anything left to look forward to anymore. Hallie was gone.

"Penny for your thoughts, Luke?" Ryder said, sliding me a beer. I sighed.

"None of them are exactly shining conversation topics."

Ryder chuckled. "That's okay. I'm still willing to give you half a cent. Then there's tax so… maybe it will end up being a quarter of a cent."

"Why don't you just give him a quarter then?" Barrett asked with a cheesy smile.

"Boo," Max stated, pushing Barrett on the shoulder as if to get rid of him. The whole thing was funny, but all I could do was, again, muster a tired smile.

"I'm upset about what happened with Hallie. I feel like I

screwed up everything. I thought we were going to be a real family, but I guess it's really not in the cards for me."

It felt weird to say it so openly like this, but the other guys were understanding. Max nodded. "It can be hard. Do you mind me asking what happened exactly?"

I sighed, because of course I minded. I didn't want everyone in the world to know what an idiot I was. But at the same time, I felt a burning need to get it off my chest.

"I was being critical, I guess. I was pushing her to submit her book to a literary agent so that she could do something with her talent. She was going to, but I guess I rushed it and made her feel like I was being controlling and judgmental. And in a way, I was."

The guys nodded, and Max offered me a reassuring smile. "We all make mistakes. Especially when we want what's best for someone we really care about."

"Not all mistakes will cost you everything," I pointed out.

"Nah, but the good ones will! The ones worth a quarter."

Again, Max pushed Barrett. He smiled and then looked at me, his expression significantly more serious. "It's actually good that you're talking about this, Luke. I'm sorry if I'm being an asshole."

I chuckled and shook my head. "You're not, it's okay. I guess I was just feeling annoyed. She wasn't really doing anything in the house. And my impression of her had always been that she had no direction."

"No direction?" Ryder asked.

I nodded. "She had a silly degree and she never told me she planned to do anything with it, so when I found out she was a writer, and a really good one at that, I could see her actually doing something with herself. But it seems like sometimes she doesn't even want to." I sighed. "I guess I just wanted more from her."

"What was your last relationship like?" he asked. "With the person you were with before Hallie, I mean."

I sighed heavily. "You mean before I caught her cheating on me with my coworker, or...?"

Barrett winced. "Ouch. I can imagine that would have made you feel reluctant to be in another relationship after that."

Max laughed. "Listen to Barrett with his honorary psychology degree."

This time, Max was pushed. "I just so happen to watch a lot of psychology videos on YouTube," Barrett said. "I could be an expert by now; you don't know."

I couldn't help but smile. Then I thought about Barrett's question and the smile faded from my lips.

"Yeah... it did make me decide that I didn't want to be in another relationship. I had been planning to propose to my ex-girlfriend and everything. Then my whole world turned upside down." I sighed. "I guess I didn't think I could find someone worth that level of risk."

"But you took a risk with Hallie, right?" Barrett encouraged.

"Look how that turned out," I grumbled, taking a swig of my beer.

"Well, yeah, but not because of her. It was because of you. Maybe you were trying to push her away."

I looked at Barrett as the idea began to take root in my mind. I had absolutely been pushing her away. It had been getting serious, and I was afraid of losing everything.

So I had gone and lost everything. I had to congratulate myself for being so efficient.

"Yeah..."

"I mean, we all have our little defense mechanisms and stuff. What were yours?" he asked.

"I guess I can be critical and judgmental, like she was

saying," I admitted. "I was always making fun of her for not having direction in her life. I wanted the best for her, but I was too hard on her. I pressured her too much to go get it. I guess it probably really hurt her."

"She triggered your defense mechanism!" Barrett exclaimed proudly. "You know it wasn't that urgent for her to get her book to an agent, but you fixated on it and pushed for it because some part of you knew it would drive her crazy."

"Maybe I did..." I said, sighing.

"No, man, you totally did! This woman is busy growing not just one, but two babies inside of her. That doesn't make her lazy, dude. It makes her a superhero. And, man, you're a doctor for crying out loud. You make more than enough money to support both of you. Sounds to me, with my super professional psychology YouTube degree, like you were just looking for an excuse to push her away."

"Yeah... I know she isn't really lazy or unmotivated. She'll figure out her career path in time. I guess part of me wanted to help her while the other part of me was afraid of actually loving her. I was acting like a big ass to her."

"That sounds about right," Barrett said as we all laughed. He raised his beer to me. We all clinked our beers and I sighed.

"I was trying to create distance between us because I guess I could tell things were getting too serious and I didn't feel like I could trust all of it yet," I said. "Man, even my own brain is against me."

Max chuckled. "You're not the only one who goes through something like this, Luke. We're only human."

Ryder nodded in agreement. "And you can only do your best with what you know at the moment. And now that you know this is something you do, you can work on it for the future."

DOCTOR'S SECRET TWINS

"There is no future left with her though. It's too late to fix it now," I said with a heavy sigh. "I was closing my heart and emotions off from her and she felt it. I made sure she did. I probably made her feel like shit about herself. I can't blame her for how she reacted to that."

"No, she was protecting herself, too, Luke. But it's not the be-all and end-all of everything. We have a lot of days ahead of us to work on things and always do better," Barrett said with a smile. "There's always hope."

Maybe there was, but if that hope wasn't with Hallie, I didn't even want it. I still was able to smile though. It was genuine this time.

"I don't know, you don't get much more assy than I was," I said with a chuckle.

"That's why you find her and seriously apologize. Explain everything you just told us. If she doesn't buy it, she doesn't buy it. But love isn't a one-way street, and if you two are meant to be together, she will give you another chance."

"Maybe..."

"Fight for her!" Max said.

"Fight!" Barrett and Ryder said in unison, holding their beers up again. I laughed and shook my head.

"Fine. I can try."

The guys all whooped in celebration, and I couldn't help but smile and shake my head. I hadn't realized how helpful it could be to talk about something like this.

I was so used to suffering alone that I guess I felt like it was the only way. Now that I had friends like this, it was strange to realize that I didn't have to anymore.

And maybe I wouldn't have to suffer either. I had to talk to Hallie.

CHAPTER 27

HALLIE

I missed Luke more with each passing day.

Missed the dimples in his chin, the way he held me when we slept, and the way he took care of me.

He really had been supportive, except when it came to my future plans.

My parents, on the other hand, were not supportive of anything.

I hated living with them. They judged and scolded me at every turn. On top of that, I had started to work longer hours at the hardware store.

That meant less time for me to focus on my writing. No time, in fact. I hadn't even gotten through two chapters in my new book.

I wanted to be with Luke, but I couldn't. I wanted to move out of my parents' house, but I couldn't afford that either. And every day being there was another reminder of what I had lost with Luke.

He lived right next door. It was impossible not to see glimpses of him sometimes. I knew his schedule and found myself watching him when he left for work, and sometimes waiting at the window to see when he came home.

It seemed a little creepy and pathetic, but I couldn't help myself. I just missed him. I wished things could have stayed the way they were.

I decided sitting alone in my room was probably not helping me get out of this mindset. I had taken to hiding out there every day after work so I wouldn't have to face my parents. But I needed some air.

I went outside to the backyard. They had a nice little garden out there that they both spent long hours landscaping. It even had a pretty gazebo with a terrace surrounding it.

I decided to sit there and look at the flowers, hoping that it might cheer me up.

Unfortunately, instead, I found my eyes drawn back to Luke's house. I wondered if he was home. I wanted so badly to just walk over there and knock on the door. I wanted him back.

It wasn't possible though. Especially not after everything that had happened. So much time had passed that he probably hated me by now.

I didn't want to cry again, but the tears began to fall. I found myself crying for everything that I had lost.

I'd lost the chance to raise the twins with Luke as a real family. To have a home where I felt safe and comfortable and loved. I'd lost the warmth in my heart when he smiled at me in that way only he had.

I'd lost the love of my life.

All of that was gone over a stupid joke and a real penchant for making me feel like a loser. I was angry at everything. At him, myself, the world. And all I could do was cry.

All I really wanted to do was to fix it and be with him

again. I could forgive him for everything if he was willing to change. But would he even be able to?

Then there was the fear of the future, now that I was pregnant. How was I ever going to manage raising two babies on my own? I had felt no fear at all when I lived with Luke. I knew that we would be able to manage it together.

But now I was alone and lost. I'd never felt more discouraged and scared in my life. I pressed my hand to my abdomen, wondering how my babies would ever forgive me for losing their father.

Having to do this alone was so hard to wrap my head around after feeling like everything was going to be taken care of. There was so much that being a single mom entailed. Could I handle it?

Or would it be another of my many failures?

Of course, he would still be there for our children. I had no doubt in my mind about that. But after the way I had just packed up and left, he would think I was an immature child.

Why wouldn't he when I ran off at the first sign of trouble? I should never have done it.

It was a good thing that I was prepared for hysterical crying. I pulled out a travel pack of tissues from my pocket and blew my nose. Being pregnant was amazing, but I could do without the hormonal sobbing.

"Are you okay?"

I nearly jumped out of my skin when I heard Luke's voice. I hadn't heard him approach over the sound of my own tears and nose-blowing. I turned to face him, my eyes wide.

"Luke?"

He gave me a gentle smile. *His* smile. "In the flesh."

God, I wished he wouldn't remind me of what he looked like in the flesh. The last thing I needed was to start grieving the sex, too.

I didn't know how to reply to that. In fact, my brain

seemed to malfunction. It had been so long since I'd been next to Luke, let alone intimate with him.

"What are you... I mean, why are you here?"

He hesitated a moment, his handsome face drawn.

"Can I sit down with you?" he asked, gesturing to the bench beside me.

I nodded. "Yeah, I guess so," I said quietly.

He smiled again at me, then stepped into the gazebo and sat down next to me. "I take it you're having a hard time," he said, gesturing to a pile of tissues at my feet.

I couldn't help but laugh sheepishly. It hadn't been the first time I'd bawled that day.

In fact, I had done it several times a week, filling the trash can in my bedroom with used tissues. He didn't need to know all of that though.

"If you're wondering about the babies, they're fine. I've been saving the ultrasound pictures and was going to mail them to you once I find a place to live."

Luke nodded slowly, then turned so his body was facing mine. "That's considerate of you," he said quietly. "You know I care about the twins, right?"

I nodded. "I know you do. You have since you found out about them."

Luke's face softened and he looked away from me for a moment. He brought his hands together. It was a nervous habit I'd noticed he had a long time ago. But he wasn't often nervous.

"Hallie, I came here today because I wanted—no, *needed*— to apologize to you."

I looked over at him, furrowing my brow. I wasn't quite sure what to expect, so I stayed quiet. I wasn't sure I could trust myself not to start crying again.

"It wasn't fair of me to treat you the way I did. I'm sorry for pressuring you to get an agent. I mean, you wrote a book all on your own, without me, and it's fantastic. I know you're clearly capable of making good decisions on your own."

I was quiet for a few moments, and then I nodded. "Thanks, Luke."

He let out a heavy sigh. "I shouldn't have been trying so hard to control your life. The truth is, I was scared. Scared of a lot of things and for a lot of reasons, so I was pushing you away."

"What were you scared of?" I asked, my voice hushed. I almost couldn't believe that this conversation was even happening.

"I was afraid of letting you in, mainly. And afraid that if I made myself vulnerable to you, maybe you would want to use me the way my ex did. She was with me more for the money and status. I guess I thought I'd feel safer if I knew you were able to take care of yourself without depending on me for my stability."

I was stunned for a moment. It stung a little that he could possibly think something like that. But considering everything he had told me about how awful his ex-girlfriend had been, it did make sense.

"I'm nothing like her, Luke."

"I know. And I've always known that. But the brain can be a little bit tricky. I thought all my concern over your career path was from a good place. I thought I was trying to encourage you to do more with yourself because I saw so much potential in you."

"You saw potential in me?" I asked.

That didn't sound accurate with how much of a hard time he liked to give me. But his eyes were sincere when he nodded.

"Absolutely. So much potential, and potential for me to be with you, that it scared me. So I was being a massive asshole. I thought it was just advice, but I could have been much more supportive. I'm sorry for dropping the ball on that one. You deserve so much better than that."

I could feel my throat tightening and I looked away, trying to blink away another waterfall of tears.

I couldn't speak, and then I felt Luke's arm around my shoulders. He was holding me gently, allowing space for me to pull away if I wanted to.

But I really didn't want to pull away. In fact, it was the very last thing I wanted.

I let him pull me close to his body. I rested my face against his shoulder and allowed myself to cry. Everything that had been building up came rushing out in that moment, when I was safe in Luke's arms.

"Everything is such a mess," I managed to say, still crying.

Luke's arms pulled me even closer, and I could feel him rubbing my back soothingly.

"Part of that is my fault, and I'm really sorry. I miss you so much, Hallie."

"I miss you too," I said, my heart feeling such a combination of things that I didn't even know what to make of it all.

He brushed the hair out of my face. Then he pulled a tissue out of the pack on the bench and offered it to me. "You have a little something on your face," he said, his eyes crinkled with a teasing smile.

I rolled my eyes and snatched the tissue away from him. I dabbed my eyes and then made sure my face was as clean as a single tissue could make it after a bout of hysterical sobbing.

He grinned. I laughed when I realized that he was already offering me another.

"Thanks," I murmured. "I didn't think you would even want to talk to me again after everything."

Luke let out a low whistle. "Same here. But you're all I've been able to think about. I want to do better, Hallie. I want us to do better together."

I nodded, my heart filling with a tentative hope for the first time since I'd left his house. "I'd like that too," I agreed. "I can't tell you how upsetting it was to think that we might not be able to be a real family."

Luke nodded but didn't speak. His expression said it all. It was clear that he had been heartbroken, too.

"I have a suggestion for you," he said, smiling at me.

"Oh, really?" I asked playfully. "Let's hear it."

"You should come over to my house. I want to make you some chicken."

I laughed. As if to betray just how good the offer sounded, my stomach growled.

"I think that was Double Trouble," I said conspiratorially. "They've been missing Daddy's cooking."

"Double Trouble?" Luke asked, his brows raised. He thought about it and then laughed. "Wait. You didn't come up with that one, did you?"

I shook my head and in unison we both said, "Tamara."

We laughed and Luke stood up, offering his hand to me. "Come on. I think the twins want to have some dinner."

I smiled and took Luke's hand. The warmth of his fingers closing around mine felt better than words could express. I had missed the comfort of his touch so much that I almost swooned.

Luke led me to his house and opened the door for me. When I walked in, I turned around and faced him in surprise.

"It's a bit of a mess," he admitted, as if he could read my thoughts. "But I'll get that all cleaned up for you."

"You've been living like a bachelor," I said, shaking my head at him in mock disapproval.

"Yeah, well, sometimes that happens when you don't have the love of your life around to keep you in line."

I blinked hard. Had he really just called me the love of his life?

When he saw my reaction, his expression softened. He stepped toward me and took both of my hands in his.

"That's right, Hallie. I love you. And I'm sorry it took me so long to figure it out."

I had been hoping I would be done with tears for the day. But once again, I found myself crying in Luke's arms. He held me close, running his hands through my hair as I calmed down.

"I love you, too," I whispered, finally pulling away to look him in the eye. "And I'm sorry too. For everything. For being a child and storming off instead of talking to you. For ignoring your calls..."

"Shhh," he said, pulling me into another warm hug. "It's okay. I know I hurt you. I'll never do anything like that again. If you can forgive me, we can move forward from this together."

I nodded. "I want that, Luke. More than anything."

"Good," he said. "Because I do too."

We held each other for a long moment. When we pulled apart, Luke's tender smile was enough to melt my entire heart.

"This is where you belong, Hallie. Right here, in this house with me. Our home."

I was swept up in emotion, but I was determined not to cry again. "But cleaner."

Luke's face brightened and he laughed jovially. "But cleaner," he agreed.

He laced his fingers through mine. "Come on," he said. "I managed to get the kitchen clean before I went to get you. I couldn't offer you dinner without at least doing that much."

I laughed as I sat down at the table. He bent down to kiss my forehead.

"Welcome home, Hallie."

CHAPTER 28

LUKE

It was like a dream come true to have Hallie back in the house. I loved seeing her every morning and being able to watch her belly grow.

But there was still work to do.

"I'm still not sure about all of this, Luke. I've got to be honest with you," Hallie said one evening as we were finishing dinner.

My heart sank, but I could understand why she would be reluctant. I'd been pretty hard on her before.

I gave her a reassuring smile. "What are you feeling right now, Hallie?"

"Well, I love being here, but I'm afraid it won't ever be enough for you."

"What do you mean?" I asked.

I felt a little on edge. All I'd wanted since she left was to have her back, but it still wasn't a sure thing. I just wished I could make her feel better.

"Well, Luke, I want to be a full-time mom to the twins. I don't want to be out there working at the hardware store. I want to be here with them, and I want to write. And the fact that I want that makes me scared and nervous because of the way you've acted."

"You don't have to be scared," I said quickly. "I want you to be happy and do the things you care about the most."

"That's the thing, Luke. I do feel like I have to be scared. You made me feel like I was an aimless, lazy person, even though I'm not. My ambitions are just different from yours. Different things make us happy. That doesn't make me a bad or lazy person."

I blew out a deep breath. "I'm sorry that what I said made you feel that way. It was a stupid thing to say."

"You wouldn't think I'm lazy even if I didn't go to graduate school? Because I don't want to do that, either."

I mustered a smile. "I don't think you're lazy for not wanting to go to grad school. In fact, this might surprise you, but I don't think you're lazy at all."

Hallie studied me for several moments. "It still scares me, Luke. I don't want us to go back to that dynamic we had before. It was hard for me. And unfair."

I felt needles in my chest and looked away for a moment. I hated hurting her. Finally, I looked back at her.

"I get that, Hallie. I really do. And I'm sorry I was so hard on you."

Hallie sighed and pushed a spoonful of potatoes around on her plate. She didn't answer or look at me. I was up to bat again.

"I should never have approached everything the way that I did. It wasn't fair to you. I was pushy and I can see how it would seem controlling."

"It *was* controlling," Hallie interjected, dropping her spoon. She finally looked up at me. She sounded mad, but she looked scared. And hurt.

"It *was* controlling," I repeated, holding my hands up in defeat. "And I'm really sorry for that. I meant well, in my head. I thought it would help you out in life for you to have a reality check. I didn't give you enough credit, though."

"You thought being arrogant would help me?"

I chuckled despite myself. "I didn't quite see it that way. But I guess that's how I was acting. It was dumb. I was operating on instinct with you, I think. I just didn't know it."

"What do you mean?" Hallie asked. Her beautiful eyes were studying me closely. I was starting to feel exposed.

I didn't really like it, but hell. Vulnerability wasn't supposed to be easy. At least not for guys like me.

"I was using my old defense mechanisms. What happened in my last relationship destroyed me, Hal. It's been so hard for me to let myself get close to you."

She continued looking at me and I sighed, trying not to betray my discomfort at opening up. But I had to do it for her.

"I didn't mean or want to be arrogant and controlling, but there was definitely part of me that didn't want to be close to you either."

She looked hurt when I said that. Her brow furrowed. "Why not?"

"It felt dangerous, in a way. Like, emotionally. It gives you the power to hurt me the way my ex-girlfriend did. I never wanted anyone else to be able to have that power."

"I think I get it," Hallie said, leaning back in her chair with a soft exhale. "I was afraid you were going to hurt me, too. It was scary to be so into someone who didn't really act like he wanted anything serious."

"I can relate to that," I said with a teasing smile. "But at the same time, I think we were both kind of just doing our best with everything. Falling for you wasn't exactly something that I ever expected."

"I think I know what you mean, but just in case…" Hallie

squinted at me, and I couldn't help but laugh at how cute she looked. "What *do* you mean?"

"I didn't expect to find someone so perfect for me. Someone who makes me feel complete in every way. Someone who complements me and softens out my hard edges."

Her face began to grow pink. I smiled and continued. "When I overheard you talking at the bar, the last thing I ever expected was to fall in love with you. But that's exactly what happened."

Her mouth dropped open. She closed it quickly, but I could tell she was getting emotional. I couldn't stop now. I wanted her to know it all.

"And now look at us. You're living in my home. You're carrying my children. All I want is to be able to take care of you and our kids for the rest of my life. I want us to be a real family, Hallie. No matter how that ends up looking."

"Even if I never get published or get a career you approve of?" she asked. Her voice was choked up. I could still sense her doubts, and I smiled gently.

"You will get published because you're an amazing writer and any agent would be stupid to turn you down. But yes, that's what I want the most, even if you don't get published or go to grad school. You mean everything to me, Hallie. And I know you're going to be an amazing mother, just like you're amazing at everything else you put your mind to."

She swallowed hard. I thought for a moment that she might break down into tears.

"Luke... you mean that?"

"I mean it, Hallie. With all of my heart. I love you. So much. And I want everything between us to work out. I'll do my part and change my old habits. I don't want to live in fear of loving you anymore. I want to embrace it. I want you."

With that, the flood of tears began. I had grown used to

her crying because of hormones, but this was different somehow.

"I love you, too," she breathed between sobs. "This has been so hard. I never want to be apart like that again."

"I know, sweetheart," I said.

I stood from my seat and went around the table to take her into my arms. I held her as she cried and dropped tender kisses on the top of her head until she calmed down.

"I love and accept you just the way you are," I said. "I'm sorry it felt like I didn't before. I'll never let that happen again. I love you, Hallie."

"I love you too," she said, uttering a soft sigh. "I think this time it's going to work, Luke."

I smiled and kissed the top of her head again. "My thoughts exactly."

CHAPTER 29

HALLIE

One Month Later

"Here we are," Luke said with a bright smile. I was dazzled again by his gorgeous blue eyes. He got out of the car and rounded it to open my door for me. "The best restaurant in Atlanta."

"Such a gentleman. I didn't know you had it in you," I teased. I stepped out of the car, and Luke used his free hand to help keep me steady.

"Oh, I'm full of surprises."

Luke dropped a quick kiss on my lips before closing the car door. He laced his arm through mine and began to lead me to the door of the gorgeous restaurant.

I'd never eaten at a place this fancy in my life. This would be a first.

Inside, the hostess greeted us.

"Reservations?"

Luke nodded. "Beckett, for two."

"Of course. Right this way."

Now, Luke's hand was holding mine with our fingers intertwined. I couldn't help but walk with a big grin on my face.

For our first official date outside of Peachwood, he was doing pretty well.

We were brought to a cozy table covered in a white tablecloth and left alone to look over the menu. Luke smiled at me.

"I have a lot of favorite foods here that I'd love you to try, but I have a feeling all you're going to want is the chicken."

I laughed and shrugged. "What can I say? Double Trouble loves poultry."

"And yet, give them eggs, and they make you throw up. Go figure."

I laughed again. It was true; the smell of eggs had made my morning sickness a whole new level of bad.

It felt good, this intimate sort of exchange with Luke. The past month had been more pleasant than I had even hoped to ask for.

I was beginning to truly feel comfortable and at peace with him. I hadn't expected it to feel so good to be freely in love with one another. Neither of us were trying to pretend otherwise, and it was such a beautiful feeling.

Once we had placed our order with the waiter, Luke reached his hand across the table and took mine. "What do you think so far? Would you consider it a fine dining experience?"

I laughed. "Ask me that after I try their fancy chicken," I said, squeezing his hand. "If it impresses the twins, it will impress me."

Luke grinned and nodded, withdrawing his hand to unfold his napkin. "Fair enough. I think I can trust my kids to distinguish truly good cooking."

"I'm sure *our* kids will have exceptional palates."

Luke nodded with mock seriousness. "Agreed."

"Do you ever miss it here?" I asked, squirming a little in my seat. Part of me was still worried he would get sick of small-town life and want to come back to Atlanta.

"I don't really think about it," Luke said with an easy laugh. "I'm actually happy to call Peachwood home these days. It's not something I expected, but all the best things in my life have happened there. I don't miss Atlanta at all."

I looked around and couldn't fight away a thought that slightly troubled me. "Did you come here a lot when you lived in Atlanta?" I asked, not daring to form the rest of my question.

"To this restaurant? You mean with Sabrina?" Luke finished for me. I blushed and looked away but nodded. He'd caught me.

"Yeah. With Sabrina."

I could feel his gentle gaze on me and ventured to look back at him.

"I mostly came here for work dinners and things like that," he said. "I brought her here a few times, but she would find something to complain about whenever I did. So I mostly kept it to myself."

"Oh…"

"Hallie, I hope you know that what I feel for you is nothing like what I felt for her. I mean, I was serious about her. I cared for and loved her. But it was nothing like what we have."

I couldn't help the drumming of my heart when I caught the intense blue of Luke's eyes looking into mine. Why was he so handsome? And so damn sincere-looking?

"I, um… haven't felt like this before either," I admitted. "It's weird. A little scary, actually."

"Scary?" Luke asked, looking suddenly troubled. "Why scary?"

"I've never had something that I already knew would destroy me if I lost it," I said with a slight laugh. "It's a different level of scary. Especially with the twins on the way."

"I don't plan on going anywhere, Hallie," Luke said. He hesitated, as if he were about to say more, but then cut himself off. "I understand that fear, though. I can't imagine losing you either."

It made me feel better to hear him say it, and I began to relax. I laughed sheepishly. "Sorry to kill the mood. I don't know why I got insecure all of a sudden."

Luke chuckled and shook his head. "Don't be sorry, Hallie. I love that you're comfortable enough to speak your mind to me about these things. But I promise you, nothing in my life has ever compared to the pleasure of meeting you."

I couldn't help but smile. "I feel that way too, Luke."

We were interrupted by the arrival of our dinners. Famished, I focused on eating. Luke looked over at me and smiled. "What do the twins think of their fancy chicken?"

I laughed. "I think they like it, but maybe one more than the other. Don't ask me how I know that."

"A mother's intuition," Luke said with warmth. I smiled and looked away.

It was so strange to me how deeply he could affect me. I liked it, though. I felt seen and heard by him.

"Well... they like it, anyway," I said, feeling a little bit flustered.

He chuckled. "And what about you?"

"What self-respecting woman would say she didn't like fancy chicken? I love it," I said. "It's a shame I have to use my table manners here, or it might just be gone by now."

Luke laughed heartily at that one. It made me grin, and

we continued eating our meals, followed by a rich slice of chocolate cake.

Our conversation was light and easy. We seemed to understand one another so well now. And it was crazy how supportive he'd become.

"So, how would you rate your first fine dining experience?" he asked as he led me back to the car. His eyes twinkled, and I felt like I could get lost in them forever.

"I really liked it," I said. "The fanciest chicken I will ever have."

Luke chuckled. "Well, now I'm starting to feel competitive. I want to make you fancy chicken."

"You don't have to. You *are* a fancy chicken."

He wrinkled his nose at me. "That doesn't even make sense."

We laughed and he opened the car door for me and waited until I was situated inside to close it again. We had a comfortable car ride back to Peachwood. I only had to stop to pee four times, which was great.

"We should take your parents there sometime," Luke said as we drove into Peachwood. "I'd love to treat them to something special."

"Like you need to win more points with them," I said with a laugh. He grinned at me.

Amazingly, my parents had grown to love Luke. He was like a part of the family now. They could clearly see he was in love with me.

Not only that, but the passion and enthusiasm he had toward our babies was touching. I had even caught my mother getting misty-eyed while he talked about our future. I don't think I could have chosen a more perfect man if I'd tried.

"I'm not trying to win points with them, Hal. I just think

they'd like it." We finally pulled into the driveway. It was good to be home. I knew where the bathroom was here.

"I know, Luke," I said, smiling over at him. "And I think it's really sweet of you. Maybe we can make plans for my mom's birthday next month."

Luke lit up. "That sounds perfect!"

When we got out of the car and I began to approach the front door, I frowned in confusion. I could hear a low murmur of voices. And Luke wasn't following me to the door. He was standing off to the side, smiling expectantly.

I blinked, then walked over to him. He waited for me to register that in the backyard, there were beautiful lights twinkling from the trees. I opened my mouth to try to form a question, but none came.

Instead, Luke offered me his arm. I took it, and we walked together to the backyard. My chest was tight when I saw it all.

The whole yard was decorated with fairy lights. Tables were adorned with gorgeous bouquets of flowers and flickering candles. It was beautiful.

I was greeted with light applause. My family, friends, and neighbors were all there, beaming at us. "What's all this?" I asked, turning around to face Luke.

But Luke wasn't where I expected him to be. Instead, he was down on one knee, and my heart crashed in my chest when I saw. His blue eyes were intense on me in the moonlight.

"Hallie..."

I brought my hands to my mouth as realization dawned on me. Was this really happening?

"For the longest time, I haven't really been able to express who I am. I was miserable. Arrogant. Even an outright jerk sometimes."

This was really happening. I pressed my hands to my heart as I listened.

"The thing about love is, it makes you want to do better. I want to be a better person for you, Hallie. I can't imagine my life without you. When I think about our family, I get so happy and excited. There's only one thing missing."

He retrieved a small velvet box from his pocket and opened it to reveal a gorgeous diamond ring. "Hallie Jones, will you marry me?"

I couldn't have stopped the tears if I tried. "Yes, Luke. Yes, I'll marry you."

Luke smiled and slipped the most gorgeous engagement ring I'd ever seen on my finger. I don't know how he managed it. I was shaking so badly.

The space erupted in applause and cheering as Luke stood up and pulled me close. We kissed deeply. I couldn't fight the tears back. I was overwhelmed in the best way possible.

He held me for an eternity before he turned to the crowd.

"We're getting married!" They cheered again, and Luke beamed at me. "I love you."

I sniffled and clung to his strong torso. "I love you, too."

"Come on. Let's go celebrate."

I nodded and the crowd welcomed us with open arms.

I was going to be Luke's wife.

And I couldn't have been happier if I tried.

CHAPTER 30

HALLIE

Two Months Later

October came so much faster than I'd expected.

I looked at my mother, who was gazing at me with tears in her eyes as we stood in the large room where we'd been getting ready.

"I always imagined what you would look like in a wedding dress, Hallie. I had no idea it would affect me this much to see it though." She laughed. "Look at me! I'm crying like a little girl."

I smiled and opened my arms up for a hug. My mom came over to me and we embraced. I could feel the waterworks coming. I was about to let loose in a sob, but Tamara bopped me on the head with a hairbrush before I could.

"Hey, we just spent an hour on that makeup. If you're going to ruin it, ruin it in front of the whole group so they can at least see we tried first."

DOCTOR'S SECRET TWINS

I laughed and wiped my eyes. My mother backed away, also chuckling.

"You seriously look so beautiful, Hallie," Whitney said, beaming at me. "Thank you so much for including me in your special day like this."

"Thank *you* for being here, Whitney. You and Ryder are like family now. I wouldn't be happy unless you were here with us."

It was true. I didn't know what I would have done the past few months without her.

Whitney and I had been friends for years, but we'd grown closer lately. Planning for the twins had been so much fun with several close friends to share it all with. I had some of the most important people in my life in the room with me now.

"Okay, champ, let's see how you look," Tamara said, offering me a hand to help me up from my chair. "I'm curious how Double Trouble likes Mama's dress."

I laughed and stood up in front of the mirror. I was shocked when I saw my reflection.

"Are you sure that's me?" I said. "I look…"

"Absolutely smokin'," Tamara interrupted.

"You look so beautiful," Whitney agreed.

"Stunning, baby," my mom added. "I'm so proud of you."

I ran my hands down my dress, letting them stop over the slight baby bump. At four months along, the twins were finally starting to show a little. Many people probably wouldn't even notice it, but those closest to me could.

"I think they approve," I said, giving my abdomen an affectionate rub. Soon, I would be officially married to their father. I had never been happier in my life. We were going to be a real family.

"Of course they do. They knew Aunt Tamara gave you the

go ahead when you found the dress. They obviously trust my immaculate taste."

She wasn't wrong. The dress was beautiful. It was elegant, but sexy.

It reached down to the ground in a full, traditional length. But the top was fun and playful. It was sleeveless and embroidered with beautiful floral patterns.

The bustline was modest, but enough to complement my ever-growing chest. I had decided against a veil, since we had come to Tybee Island and I didn't want the wind to blow it around. But I was wearing a beautiful headpiece that made me feel like some kind of goddess.

"I love the dress," I said.

"Great. Unfortunately, you screwed over the bridesmaids like a typical bridezilla. You know purple isn't my color. I'm a redhead!"

I snorted and Tamara grinned. "I'm just kidding, Hal. The dresses are beautiful."

I had already known she was kidding. She'd helped me choose them. They were sleeveless too. They reached just above the knee, with golden accents.

"Seriously though, you're so, so beautiful," Tamara said. "Luke is such a lucky guy."

"I'm lucky, too," I said with a soft sigh. "I never would have imagined my life turning out like this."

We all smiled and piled in for a group hug.

"All right, Hal. It's about that time now," Whitney said, glancing at her watch. "Are you ready?"

The nervous butterflies that had been living in my stomach since Luke proposed began to flutter around. I nodded, though I was incredibly nervous. "Yeah. Let's do this."

Whitney nodded and we headed out the door. My mother walked beside me, and she surprised me by taking my hand.

"Hallie, I know that we've had our differences over Luke and everything else. But I want you to know that I'm so proud of the woman you've become. I know you're going to take everything you want from this life, and it's everything you deserve. That's all I've ever really wanted for you. Just to be happy."

I swallowed the lump in my throat, and my mom hugged me just before we made it to the chapel on the beach where the ceremony was taking place.

Everyone was gathered inside. Tamara walked down the aisle, followed by Whitney and then Mom.

My father approached me with a smile.

"You look beautiful, kiddo," he said.

"Thanks, Dad."

"I'm proud of you, Hallie."

I grinned. My parents' acceptance meant the world.

Finally, I took my place as the music changed. Luke caught my eye and gasped, which made me smile.

"Ready?" Dad winked and offered me his arm.

"Ready."

Dad walked me down the aisle, and I held Luke's gaze the whole time. Finally, when we reached the altar, Luke took my hand. His eyes held so much love for me that all my nervousness slipped away.

The priest began to speak. I could barely register any of the words being said. All I could do was stare at Luke. He was my rock, and I focused on him.

Finally, it came time for the rings. I smiled at little Eden, who had begged to be our ring bearer, and we exchanged rings. My heart thudded hard in my chest when Luke took my hand and put the ring on my finger. I slipped his on, and then we held hands until it was time to kiss.

"I love you so much," Luke murmured before pressing his lips against mine. I held him tightly, so happy and grateful that I was marrying the love of my life. It was more than I had ever hoped for.

"I love you, too."

~

The honeymoon was just as magical. The next morning, I woke up to find that Luke wasn't in bed. Figuring that he was out exploring while I slept in, I decided to sneak to my laptop to get some writing done while he was busy. I had a few finishing touches to put on a chapter and was eager to finish.

After a quick session of work, I got dressed. Luke had left me a sweet note on the mirror telling me that he was going to be on the beach. I grinned and ran out to find him.

When I spotted him, I ran to him. He swept me up in his arms and ran with me to the ocean as if he were about to throw me in.

"No, you can't do that to me," I exclaimed with a laugh. "I'm carrying your children."

"They have to learn to swim sometime," Luke said with a bright smile.

But thankfully, he didn't toss me in. Instead, he held me close so he could kiss me deeply. God, he felt good.

"It's a little too early for that, if you ask me. I don't think a uterus counts as a floatie."

Luke snorted and set me back down on my feet. He brought his hand to my stomach and ran his thumb along it, smiling gently.

"You know we're going to have to name them eventually."

I smiled. "There's enough time for that."

He nodded and led me to the blanket he'd set up on the beach. There was a big umbrella that he ushered me beneath. He was so protective of me that it was almost cute.

"Did you sleep well?" he asked, sitting down beside me. His eyes were such a bright blue in the sun that I almost couldn't find my voice.

"I did. I finished a chapter, too."

Luke laughed heartily. "You work even on your honeymoon. Man, I sure had you pegged wrong when we first met."

I laughed. "Good thing you did, or we might not be here right now."

Luke grinned. "Good thing you liked me enough to give me a second chance."

I swatted at him. "I think we would have ended up here either way," I admitted. "It feels like it was fated."

He took my hands in his and smiled. "I feel that way too, Hal. I'm so happy to be with you. I can't believe you're my wife now!"

"Mrs. Beckett," I said, testing the name. I had considered keeping my last name, or hyphenating it, but something in me really liked taking his name. So that's what I did. We'd all have the same last name in the family.

I didn't think there was anything wrong with keeping my name, but it just felt good to have it that way. Comfortable.

"Well, Mrs. Beckett. How do you feel about taking a walk along the beach with me?" Luke asked, running his hand down my arm. It brought goosebumps along the flesh where he touched.

"I think that sounds amazing, Dr. Beckett."

Luke grinned and offered me a hand. We stood up together and I grinned.

"Race you!" I said. I started running, then burst out laughing when Luke suddenly picked me up from behind and kept running.

"Oh, no, it looks like a tie," he said once we made it to the water's edge. I laughed and he set me down but didn't let go.

He hugged me close to him and we fell into a deep, sensual kiss.

When we finally broke apart, my heart was hammering in my chest, and I had half a mind to go back to the hotel room right then and there.

Luke seemed to be able to read my mind.

"Race you," he murmured.

CHAPTER 31

HALLIE

"Are you okay?" Luke asked me with wide eyes for the thousandth time that day. I laughed and shook my head.

"I was just stretching, Luke. That was my stretchy noise."

Luke didn't look entirely convinced and kept his worried gaze fixed upon me. I sighed and shook my head at him. "Seriously, Luke. I promise. You will be the first to know when I'm in labor."

"I just want to make sure you're all okay."

"I promise I'm fine. And so are the boys."

Luke beamed. "I can't believe we're going to have sons. It's going to be so much fun."

I smiled and nodded in agreement. "You're right, it will. I can't wait either."

It would have been amazing to have girls, too. But discovering the sex of the twins had been such exciting news. We had been able to really think about naming them and trying to work out how to set up the nursery.

Luke had been doing his best to keep himself busy by working on converting the guest bedroom into a nursery. He had been doing an amazing job. The room was painted lemon yellow and decked out with blue accents.

"I can't believe your coworkers pitched in to get that really expensive nursery set for us," I said, shaking my head. "I never would have expected something like that."

It was so beautiful. I had been surprised by a baby shower a few weeks ago, and we'd been going through the gifts and assembling furniture since then. I was overwhelmed by the generosity and support of my family and friends.

Then again, that was why I loved Peachwood. It was a real, true community. We grew together here.

I was so happy I was going to be raising a family in a place like this. And even more happy that Luke was excited to do the same. He'd been so standoffish about the small-town atmosphere that for a while, I feared he'd want to return to Atlanta.

But he didn't. He had told me that he wanted to stay, and he meant it. I couldn't have been happier.

"By the way, my parents need me to train Ariel as store manager at the hardware store today," I said.

Whitney's sister took my old position at the hardware store. I hadn't worked there much since I'd moved back in with Luke. Helping my parents out to train Ariel was the least I could do.

Luke looked uncomfortable but nodded. "Okay. Just take it easy and let me know if you need anything."

"I will. I promise. Besides, my parents are usually there or just a phone call away."

"I'm just a phone call away, too, you know."

"I know," I said, going over to Luke and kissing him.

He had been so anxious that I was almost impatient for the twins to be born just so he would relax a little. It felt like I couldn't so much as snore in bed without him poking at me to check to see if I was okay.

DOCTOR'S SECRET TWINS

That afternoon, I was at the hardware store, smiling at the spitting image of Whitney. "All right. I'll show you the basics. Let me know at any point if you have any questions."

Ariel smiled and nodded. She was sweet. I could see why my parents had chosen her after their long process of trying to find a suitable manager.

"I will! It's going to be a lot different from my last job. I was getting a little burned out dealing with cranky patients at the physical therapy office."

I laughed. Ariel had managed a PT office, and I knew the job had been stressful for her. She also knew her way around the hardware store, since she was no stranger to home repair projects with her young family.

"I can imagine. I'm sure you'll like it here. I think you're a perfect fit, honestly. And I promise, it's not as grueling as a lot of jobs can be. You just have to know your power tools to stay on my dad's good side." I laughed.

"Then I should fit right in," she said brightly.

"I have no doubt in my mind that you will," I said with a grin.

I winced suddenly as a spike of pain shot through my abdomen.

"Are you okay?" Ariel asked, knitting her brow together.

"Yeah, just a weird cramp," I said with a laugh. "I've been getting Braxton Hicks lately. I had no idea being pregnant would be such an ordeal."

Ariel smiled. "Tell me about it. I've been there twice," she said with a chuckle. "How is your book deal going?"

I beamed. "It's been amazing, actually! My publisher is already getting on me about a second book for the series."

"That's incredible!" Ariel exclaimed. "I'm so proud of you, Hallie. Peachwood's own author."

I smiled. "Thank you! It's pretty exciting, honestly. I never thought this could happen. But here I am."

"That's so cool. I love that you can do what you're passionate about. You're such a talented writer."

"I appreciate that. I know you guys have already read it, but the official release date is next month! I will be a published author soon."

"Exciting!"

Another sudden, much more severe pain nearly knocked the wind out of me. Ariel frowned. "Are you sure those are fake labor contractions?"

I couldn't even reply as the pain was too great. Instead, I took my phone out and texted Luke to tell him about it.

Not long after I put my phone down, Luke was coming through the door in a panic. I almost laughed, but the pain was too distracting.

Luke ushered me out the door and led me toward the car. Just before we made it, I felt my water break. "Oh, boy," I breathed.

"This is it," he said, his eyes wide. He helped me into the car and took off toward the hospital at a speed I was certain was illegal on just about every road in Peachwood. "Just stay calm! I'll take care of you."

The contractions were beginning to come closer together now. The pain was far more intense. I caught my breath and glanced over at him.

"I think… maybe… *you* ought to calm down."

He glanced over at me sheepishly but didn't slow down. We made it to the hospital in record time. He made sure I got into a room as quickly as possible, and soon my obstetrician was with us.

"How is she?" Luke demanded. "And the twins? Are they going to need a cesarean? Because I know twins often bring complications…"

Dr. Reynolds held up a hand and chuckled softly. "Everything is fine. They're in the prime position for a vaginal birth. Not to worry, Dr. Beckett. Your family is doing just fine."

Luke let out a breath but nodded. He ran a hand through his hair, then took his place beside me and held my hand. His hand was shaking slightly, and I squeezed it.

The birth went a lot faster than anyone expected. There was no time for an epidural, and I dilated quickly. All I could do was grit my teeth and go along with the ride.

It was very painful, and Luke helped me focus on my breathing. He tried to stay calm for me, but I could tell he was on edge. I was sure at one point that he might pass out, but he stayed strong.

When the time came to push, he held both my hands. It was agonizing, but I managed to do it.

As soon as my sons were born, I forgot all about the pain.

Soon, I heard Dr. Reynolds chuckle. "One boy," she confirmed. "Happy and healthy." She handed the baby to a nurse, who checked the baby's vitals, and I heard a soft cry. My heart swelled in my chest and I bore down to push again.

The doctor lifted the second baby up where I could see him. "Two boys."

A second cry filled the room just as I was handed one of the babies. Before long, the other was in my arms.

I closed my eyes and let my shoulders shake with the sob that overtook me. I hadn't been prepared for the overwhelming love I felt from having them in my arms for the first time.

"They're beautiful," Luke whispered, holding his arm around me. I nodded and wanted to reply, but I was too choked up with emotion. I hadn't expected this at all. "And so tiny…"

I nodded, tears falling down my cheeks. "They're perfect."

"Hi, Silas," Luke said, pressing a finger into our eldest's

tiny hand. The little fingers curled around his large finger. I'd never seen him smile more intensely.

"Hi, Wesley," I said, pressing a soft kiss against the younger baby's head. Then I kissed Silas, too.

"Thank you, Hallie. You did it, and I'm so proud of you," Luke whispered. He looked at me, his expression so full of adoration that more tears formed in my eyes. "I've never loved you more."

I smiled and watched as Luke gently lifted one of the babies from my arms. I was so grateful.

We were a family.

EPILOGUE

HALLIE

Three Months Later

"Can I hold him?" Eden exclaimed. "I'm good with babies."

"I know you are," I said with a soft chuckle. "Come sit up here next to me. I'll let you hold Silas, but Wesley is having fun with Ryder right now."

"Does Uncle Ryder know that Wesley won't remember how to barbeque even though he's trying to teach him?" Eden asked seriously.

We all laughed, and I nodded. "I'm sure he won't be offended if the baby doesn't remember. His daddy can show him if he forgets."

"Okay."

I gently lowered the baby into Eden's arms, and she beamed. I kept my hands under her arms as support, but she held the baby expertly and carefully as he cooed and kicked his legs.

The babies had such a pleasant and friendly temperament. When Luke had suggested hosting a Fourth of July barbeque at our house, I had been a little concerned about having them around so many people at once. To my surprise, the twins loved it.

"How will you tell them apart?" Eden asked. "They're iden-ti-bul."

Sage laughed. "Identical, honey."

Eden shrugged. "Right. They look exactly the same!"

I laughed. "It can be hard, but I can tell. They have different personalities. Wesley is more active and louder, and Silas is a little more calm."

I lifted Silas's leg to reveal a small birthmark on the back of his thigh. "And if all else fails, Silas has this birthmark, and Wesley doesn't."

Eden giggled. "That's funny! I bet they'll play pranks on you when they get bigger."

"I'm already counting on that. Especially knowing their father." I laughed.

"They're so perfect, Hallie," Sage said with a wistful smile. "Thank you for having us all over. It's been too long since I saw the twins last."

"I'm glad I did. I wanted to have everyone over sooner, but—"

"Oh, honey, say no more. There's a whole process after giving birth. You take whatever time you need. Nobody will question that."

I smiled. "It seems kind of full circle, doesn't it? It's been a year since Luke and I met. And now, here we are."

"Isn't it wild how life changes like that?" Penny said with a chuckle.

"It really is. I never would have imagined my life would take a turn like this."

"And you're a published writer now, too!" Mom said,

shaking her head. "My daughter, the author. I still can't believe you never told us you were writing a book!" She looked at Tamara. "And you never said a word, either."

Tamara held her hands up in defense. "She swore me to secrecy."

I laughed. "Well, it all worked out in the end."

"I'll say," Whitney said. "Your book is all the other nurses can talk about at the hospital." She smiled. "You've done well for yourself this year, Hallie. A successful book and two beautiful babies."

"And a beautiful husband," I added, smiling at Luke where he stood near the grill across the yard.

Ryder handed Wesley back to Luke, who held the baby securely. My heart warmed at the sight. How could I possibly have gotten so lucky?

"He's all right," Tamara said, wrinkling her nose. I laughed and swatted at her. I knew she was joking—she'd grown to appreciate my husband once she saw how good he was for me.

Silas began to shift and fuss, so I gently picked him up from Eden's arms. "Come here, baby. I think it's time to change your diaper."

I smiled at my friends and mother. I couldn't have gotten to where I was now without their support the past few months, especially since my parents had welcomed Luke into the family.

Everything had fallen into place better than I could have dreamed.

All it took was listening to my heart and taking a chance on love.

"Be right back." I stood and walked over to Luke. He looked up at me with a grin. "I'm going to go check their diapers," I said to him.

"Let's do it." He smiled as he followed me inside.

Luke was a devoted dad. He wanted to do everything he could for us. It had shocked me at first. But I loved it, and I loved him more every day.

We stood side by side in the nursery to change the babies. Luke murmured gently to them as we worked. When we were finished, we picked the twins up and stood together in a comfortable silence. Luke wrapped an arm around me and held me close.

It was the perfect moment. Luke and I were in love with our babies and each other.

"Guess we should get back out there," I finally said, shifting Silas in my arms.

"Just one thing first," Luke said. I looked at him curiously.

"What's that?"

He smiled and pressed a gentle kiss against my lips. "I love you."

I beamed and took his hand. "I love you, too."

"I don't think life could be any more perfect than this."

And he was right.

Thank you for reading! If you liked this book, you'll LOVE **Boss's Secret Baby.**

It's the sexy, heartwarming story of second chances, true love, and big surprises.

My new boss is my baby's daddy...
He just doesn't know it yet.

But when he sees my son for the first time...
Feels a fatherly connection that he can't describe,
He knows something is wrong.

**I have a secret that's four years old.
And that secret needs a daddy.**

This full-length romance is full of heart and heat! You'll love Carter and Isabelle's story, and the ending will leave you more than satisfied. :)

Grab your copy of Boss's Secret Baby here!

SNEAK PEEK OF BOSS'S SECRET BABY!

ABOUT THE BOOK

My new boss is my baby's daddy...
He just doesn't know it yet.

But when he sees my son for the first time...
Feels a fatherly connection that he can't describe,
He knows something is wrong.

Five years ago, Carter and I had one unforgettable night hours before he left town.
I tried to find him, but fate had other plans.

Now, five years later, he's back in town.
And my baby's daddy is my prick of a new boss.

The moment his intense soul piercing blue eyes lock on mine,
I know I'm in trouble.

I have a secret that's four years old.
And that secret needs a daddy.

Hopefully Carter needs a mama...

Can our second chance survive a secret this big?

Grab your copy of Boss's Secret Baby here!

CHAPTER 1

Isabelle

Five Years Ago

"Are you kidding me?" I cried out, staring at Ryan.

He sat back in his chair, nonchalant as hell, looking like he hadn't just ripped my whole world apart.

"Come on, babe. It's better this way."

I shook my head. I couldn't wrap my mind around the fact that Ryan had taken me out on a date night just to break up with me. Who arranges a break-up date?

"How is it better?" I asked, trying not to let my voice tremble or to sound like I was going to cry. Which was exactly what I felt like doing. "We've been together for two years, and you're just throwing it all away."

"I'm not throwing it all away, babe." He leaned forward, reaching for my hand over the table.

"Don't call me that," I said, snatching my hand away before he could touch me. "You're dumping me. You can go right back to using my name."

"Fine, Isabelle," Ryan said, making my name sound like it

tasted bad in his mouth. "I'm trying to be nice here, but you're not being very open to me right now."

I barked a sarcastic laugh. "You're right, how thoughtless of me. I'll take notes so next time you dump me, I'm more gracious about it."

He sighed. "Don't be like this."

I crossed my arms over my chest. "I'll be however the hell I want. You don't get to make demands anymore."

He shrugged. "Okay. Sure. I guess you're right."

Damn straight I was right. Ryan was dumping me. I suddenly realized there was no reason I had to be here. He'd said his piece—we were over. He'd already explained that he wasn't ready to make a commitment. There was nothing left for me to do or say here.

I stood to leave.

"Wait," Ryan said. "We're not going Dutch on the check?"

My mouth dropped. "Get the check yourself, asshole." I turned and marched away from him.

I bit back my sobs until I was out of the bar where we'd met, and at least halfway down the road to the bus stop. When the tears finally rolled down my cheeks, a sob racked my throat.

I fished for my phone and called June.

"He dumped me," I sobbed into the phone.

"What? Izzy, oh, my God!"

"I know," I said. "He invited me out for drinks. We had a beer, and then we ate that greasy pub food I love so much. And then he dumped me. After we'd had a good afternoon together."

"I can't believe it," June said. "I have to get Bernie into this call, too."

I nodded, waiting for June to dial Bernadette into the call so we were on a three-way. My two best friends were saints, always there for me when shit hit the fan.

And shit had just hit the fan in a big way.

We were all in college together. I was in the art program, June studied communications and Bernie was going to be a teacher, but we'd shared a dorm room the first year and we'd been attached at the hip ever since.

"Izzy, are you okay?" Bernie asked when she hopped on the line. "June told me before connecting me."

"I'm fine," I lied. I felt like collapsing on the curb in a puddle of tears.

"He doesn't deserve you," Bernie said fiercely.

"I stuck him with the check this time. We usually split it," I said.

For some reason, I felt bad about doing that. But that was my problem—I was too nice. I always ended up getting walked over because I didn't want people to go out of their way for me. So, I ended up putting myself second.

All the time.

I was a secondary character in my own story when I should have been the main character who took all the glory.

And this just proved it. Not even Ryan wanted to be with me anymore.

"It's good you made him pay," June said. "I wish you could have stuck it to him more, really made his life hell somehow."

Bernie agreed.

"I don't want to make his life hell," I said. "I just... want to move on."

That wasn't going to be so easy. I was still fixated on Ryan. Hell, until half an hour ago, I hadn't even known anything was wrong between us. I was starting my last year at college, and he finished last year. We'd been talking about moving in together, planning a future. I'd been ready for the long haul with him.

And he hadn't been able to see past today.

I swallowed down a sob.

"Do you know what you need?" June asked. "A rebound," she added before I could guess. "You need to get out there and get in bed with a hottie that will make you forget all about that idiot."

"Excellent idea! Don't waste any time on that loser," Bernie agreed enthusiastically.

"I don't know, you guys…" I wasn't really the type to sleep around. I was a long-term relationship gal through and through. One-night stands weren't my thing.

"We should go out," Bernie suggested. "We can drown your sorrows in alcohol. When you're too drunk to judge if the guy is hot enough to take home with you, we'll help you decide." She sounded triumphant.

"I'm working tonight," I said.

I reached the bus stop and glanced at the other people waiting to get on board. There were only two. One had earphones in his ears, and wouldn't hear my conversation. The other was reading a book.

"Come on," June groaned. "Cancel your shift."

"I can't do that. Besides, I'm saving up money for…" I didn't know how to finish that sentence. I'd been saving so Ryan and I could get an apartment after I graduated. Now, that wasn't going to happen. But I would still need a place to stay, whether it was with him or not. My stomach turned and I felt sick. God, all of this was so unexpected. And so unfair.

The bus rumbled toward us.

"I have to go," I said. "I'm working my shift, and then I'm going to bed. We'll talk tomorrow."

The girls protested for a short while longer, but then they gave in, and I ended the call. I climbed onto the bus, feeling numb, and I sat in a seat near the back. I leaned my head against the window and watched the city slide by as the bus snaked through the streets of Los Angeles, taking me back to my student housing.

My shift at Café Noir started at five, and it ran until one in the morning. The café was a simple place during the day, offering food and artisan coffee. At night, we whipped out the cocktail menus and craft beers, and the crowd shifted from sensible daytime workers to raucous students.

I liked working there—it always had a good vibe, and since I'd worked at the café almost as long as I'd been studying, it felt like a home away from home.

"Hey, Izzy," my coworker Jimmy said when I clocked in for my shift and he clocked out. "Are you okay? You look…"

"I'm okay," I said before he could finish his sentence. "Just a tough week with classes and tests."

"You have some days off coming up soon, right? Then you can rest," he said.

"Yeah, that's true," I agreed. He gave me a sympathetic smile before he left.

I walked to the counter, ready to serve the customers coming in for the late afternoon rush, and tried not to think about Ryan at all.

It would be no use if I cried into someone's coffee. That was just unprofessional.

Time ticked on and the orders changed from coffee to cocktails when the dinner orders started coming in. I worked hard, running back and forth, focusing on work so that I didn't have to think about anything else. My mind kept jumping to Ryan, and when I forced it away, I thought about what June and Bernie had suggested—a rebound. But I couldn't do that.

Could I?

I'd been in a two-year relationship until today. I'd been thinking long term. My mind had been on the future, not on the present, and not on getting my physical needs met. Instant gratification had been the last thing I'd wanted.

I felt like the rug had been ripped out from under me.

"Two black coffees, and the best stout you have on tap," a deep voice said. I looked up.

Oh. My. God.

The bluest eyes I'd ever seen pierced me, and they were set in a face that could only have been carved by the angels. He was the epitome of tall, dark, and handsome, with tanned skin that made him look like he went for morning runs on the beach, broad shoulders, a confident attitude, and a grin on his face that made my stomach flutter.

"Coming right up," I managed to say, which was a damn miracle because the sight of Mr. Hot-as-Hell had made me feel tongue-tied. I turned away from him to prepare his order. Two coffees and a stout—that was the order, right? Good thing he'd said it before I'd seen his face because I wouldn't have heard a word he said.

What was wrong with me? I didn't usually notice guys like this. But if they looked like him, I'm sure I would have looked twice. Relationship or not.

When I'd prepared the two coffees, I put them on the counter.

He smiled at me and my heart skipped a beat.

"Let me just get that beer," I said.

He nodded, and I walked to the beer taps to pour the stout. I took the pint glass to the counter and put it down, calculating the price in my mind.

He pulled out a handful of bills and smiled at me again.

Cue the butterflies.

"Keep the change," he said.

"Thanks. Here you go," I said, offering him a tray for the coffee and the beer so that he wouldn't have to juggle them all.

"Thanks," he said. He flashed me that grin and walked away.

The conversation had been simple. But I shivered, my

stomach tightening again, and I watched him walk to a table with another man and a woman.

My stomach sank a little. Was he taken?

I snuck glances at him the rest of the night while I worked, watching the body language of his group. They were too far away from the counter for me to hear what they were saying, and as the evening picked up and I got busier, I could focus on them less and less. But at some point, the other man leaned over and kissed the woman, and I was oddly satisfied.

They were a couple. Mr. Dreamy was a third wheel.

Which didn't mean he was definitely single—a man that attractive had to have a woman who was supermodel material. But still, a girl could hope.

They stood and left, and my stomach sank again when the table was empty. I would have liked to at least talk to him again.

But men like him didn't happen to women like me.

Just as well. I didn't need to get hurt another time.

It would have been nice, though, if at least one thing in my life worked out the way it did in the movies. Since I'd already lost my happy ending and all, I was due for some sort of good luck.

I wiped down the counter while I waited for the next person to order. It was close to midnight and business was dying down. We were closing up soon. And then I had to clean up before I could go home.

Someone walked up to the counter and cleared his throat.

When I looked up, I froze. Once again, I was caught in the gaze of Mr. Blue Eyes.

CHAPTER 2

Carter

Fuck, she was cute. Not just cute, smoldering hot, too. But something about the way she looked at me, the way her mouth perpetually looked like it wanted to curl into a smile, made me want to talk to her.

"Hi, Isabelle," I said when she looked up at me, blinking like I was some kind of vision.

She glanced down at her name tag, which was where I'd found out her gorgeous name. Then she looked back up at me.

"Hi," she said. "Can I… can I get you something? I think our kitchen is closed, but…" She looked over her shoulder at the kitchen. She was flustered, and that made her even more attractive.

And she was already a stunner, with red hair that hung over her shoulder in light curls, and big, round brown eyes that made me want to fall into them.

"Yeah," I said. "Your number."

She blinked at me. "What?"

"I'm a little forward," I said. "Sorry about that. You're just the most beautiful thing I've seen in a long, long time. And I can't pass up the opportunity to spend some time with you."

She blinked at me before her cheeks flushed.

"I'm not a thing," she bristled.

I laughed. Oh, God. Feisty, too. She was the whole package.

"I just told you you're beautiful, and all you heard was that I said thing?"

She shrugged. "I don't like being treated like the help."

I laughed again. "I wasn't trying to treat you like the help. Poor choice of words. You're the most beautiful woman I've seen in a long, long time. Is that better?"

She bit her lip, then nodded shyly.

Shit. Already, she was driving me wild. I smiled.

"I want to spend some time with you. Would you like to have a drink with me?"

She hesitated.

"There's still time before you close, right?" I asked.

"I'm not allowed to drink on the job," she said.

"Who's going to know?" I asked. "We're the only ones left."

When she looked around, she saw I was right. There weren't any other patrons left. Everyone had gone home for the night. It was five minutes to twelve, and there was still time for her to pour another couple of beers.

She turned it over in her mind. I could see her thinking. And it was hot as hell.

"Okay," she finally said.

I grinned at her. "Okay."

She disappeared and a moment later, she returned with two beers.

We walked to the table where I'd sat with my college pal, Ray, and his girlfriend, Sonya.

"So, Isabelle," I said when we sat down.

"Most people call me Izzy," she said. "The name tag is formal." She touched her fingers to the tag on her chest.

"Izzy." Sassy. I liked it. "I'm Carter."

She smiled. "Hi, Carter."

I smiled at the sound of my name on her lips.

"So, Izzy, what do you do? Besides work here?"

"I'm a student," she said. "Art major."

I whistled through my teeth. "That's impressive."

"Is it?"

"For sure," I said. She looked shy under the compliment.

I had a lot of respect for art students. It was a difficult career path—it was all about passion to them because most of them didn't make it far in the art world. Making money from something like that, no matter how passionate you were about it, was hard.

"What about you?" she asked.

"I finished college last year. I'm just wrapping up an internship now."

"So, what's next for you, then?" she asked.

I took a swig of beer. "Business school."

"Really?"

I nodded. "I want to make a difference, you know? But not in the way most people say they want to."

"How, then?"

"Gourmet food."

She laughed, and I was in trouble. I could get addicted to that sound.

"Hey," I said, poking her lightly in the shoulder and loving the contact. "Good food brings people together. And it makes a profitable business, too."

"I like your enthusiasm. Where's your school?" she asked.

"New York."

Was it my imagination, or did her face fall?

I was flying out to New York City in two days to start graduate school. I'd worked hard to get where I was now, and I'd work even harder when I got to the Big Apple.

"When are you leaving?" she asked.

I hesitated, unsure if I should tell her. I didn't want to scare her off.

"In two days."

Her eyes widened. "Oh, that's soon."

I nodded.

Leaving was bittersweet. I loved LA, but I needed to take this next step. An MBA would open a lot of doors for me. And I had big plans.

"Well, I'm sure you'll do well in grad school," Izzy said. "It sounds like you're passionate about your future business."

I nodded. "Absolutely. What's the point if there's no passion?"

"Exactly," she said. "That's why I'm studying art, even though I know what most people say about it."

"I think it's noble," I said. "What kind of art do you make?"

"I'm a painter," she said, her eyes lighting up.

"Ah. What do you like to paint?"

"Anything," she said, playing with a lock of her fire-red hair. "Landscapes, abstract. But portraits are my favorite. I love people's faces. They always tell a story."

She smiled at me. Her eyes were mesmerizing. I knew I was leaving soon, but I wanted to get to know her better. Something about her made me want to get closer, to find out what made her tick.

"Are you single?" I asked.

My question surprised me as much as it surprised her.

"Yeah," she said, and an expression flickered across her face too fast for me to read.

"Lucky me," I said and grinned at her.

She laughed, and it was beautiful. Rich and full and genuine.

"Yeah, I guess you are."

I took a sip of my beer. "So, what are you doing when you're not working at Café Noir or painting pictures?"

"Being a full-time student and working take up most of my time," she admitted.

"What are you doing tonight?" I asked.

She shrugged. "After locking up and erasing all signs of my breaking the rules right now—" she winked at me "—I'm probably going to go home and get a good night's sleep so that I'm up early for classes again tomorrow."

"That's too bad," I said.

"Why?"

"Because I was hoping you would come out with me to celebrate."

She blinked at me. "What are we celebrating?"

"The fact that I met the most beautiful woman I've ever seen." I grinned at her and watched as she blushed bright red.

"Oh, you are smooth, Carter. But meeting me is hardly cause for celebration."

"Oh, Isabelle," I said, leaning forward. "Have you *seen* you?"

She blushed again and I reached forward, touching her arm. I couldn't help myself. She was magnetic.

"So, what do you say?" I asked. "When you're done here, do you want to come with me?"

"Where are we going?" she asked in a breathy voice.

"Wherever you want."

"For someone who looks so put together, I'd think you'd have an answer ready for that question," she said.

I laughed. "You think I look put together?"

"Don't you?" she asked. "I mean, look at you." She slid her eyes over my body, and I relished the way she looked at me. "You're definitely the type of guy to command a boardroom."

I laughed. "Is it that obvious that I'm a business major? I couldn't pass for a carpenter, or a lumberjack?"

She raised her eyebrows. "Seriously? A lumberjack? I can just picture you in flannels and boots, sizing up a tree, wondering how much you'll have to bribe it to fall over for you."

I burst out laughing. "Bribe it?"

"Well, I can tell you work out," she said, blushing. "But you don't have the callused hands of someone who runs a chainsaw for a living." She reached for me and took my hand in both of hers. At the contact, electricity jumped between us and my breath caught in my throat. She glanced up at me before studying my hand.

I loved the feel of her hands on mine, her skin soft and smooth, and her fingers able. She had paint spots on her hands, and the splotches were endearing.

I leaned forward so that our heads were bowed together, studying my hand.

"So, you think I'll be better at closing deals than chopping down trees?" I asked. My voice was a little hoarse.

She glanced up at me again and her face was so close to mine, I could see the flecks of gold dancing in those big brown eyes.

"Yeah. And it's better for the environment."

I chuckled. I could smell her shampoo. I lifted my free hand and tucked her hair behind her ear. Her eyes were locked on mine, and when I leaned in to kiss her, she closed her eyes.

When our lips touched, it was the same incredible electrical surge that pulsed through me as when she'd touched my hand. I slid my tongue into her mouth and she moaned softly.

The sound was erotic, and it made my cock stiffen in my pants.

I cupped her cheek and kissed her more urgently, trying to show her the effect she was having on me. I moved my hands to her back, sliding them over her shoulders and up to her hair as I pulled her closer. Her arms wrapped around my shoulders. I inhaled her scent, intoxicated.

When we finally broke apart to look at each other, she was out of breath as if she'd run a mile, and her eyes were darker, deeper. Her lips were slightly parted.

"Come home with me," I said.

She leaned back a little.

Shit, did I blow it?

"I have to clean up and lock up the café," she said.

I nodded. "I'll help you."

We stood together. All the other employees had gone home, and I helped her close up. We tipped the chairs onto the tables for the cleaning crew to come in the morning, wiped the counters down, and she switched on the large industrial dishwasher that someone had loaded earlier.

The whole time, I couldn't stop staring at her. I watched her as she moved, keeping track of her as we worked. She was elegant and graceful, doing everything with care, as if it really mattered. Her long red hair was like a flame as she moved beneath the dim lights. When she glanced at me now and again, her eyes were deep. Her expression suggested she was as eager about getting out of here as I was.

When the shop was ready, and she'd locked the door, she turned to me.

"I don't usually do this," she announced.

"What? Have help cleaning up the shop?"

She giggled. "No. Go home with someone I just met. It's not usually… my style."

"Okay," I said. What if she changed her mind? I desperately needed her, but I didn't want to persuade her to do something she didn't want. "Are you sure you want to do this?"

"Yes, I am. But I just wanted you to know that."

I nodded. "Noted. And I'm honored."

"So, which way?" she asked.

I took her hand and lifted it to my mouth, brushing my lips against her knuckles.

"This way," I breathed and led her to my car.

CHAPTER 3

Isabelle

I was going home with him.

I hardly recognized myself. A one-night stand? And what was more, I was fresh out of a long-term relationship. That was who I was— the long-term relationship girl.

Where had that gotten me?

Dumped and feeling like crap because Ryan didn't think I was good enough to commit to.

And that was bullshit.

Maybe I wasn't like some of the other girls around campus, who had a ton of friends and big trust funds, but I had some good things going for me.

And Carter could see that. He talked to me like I was worth something.

I realized that for a long time, Ryan had made me feel like I wasn't worth much. I had been so caught up in our dream of 'forever' that I hadn't noticed how he'd started disregarding me.

He'd started treating me like I was a maybe in his life, when he'd been a definitely in mine all that time.

Carter looked at me like I was the only woman in the world. Even though it was just for tonight, the way he treated me felt good.

We rode with the windows down. He moved his hand to my leg and interlinked his fingers with mine. It was sexy, but sweet, too. Everything about him, every little move he made, was perfect.

His car was nice. Expensive, but not in a flashy way. I liked that about him—he was obviously higher on the economic food chain, and he had a few doors already open for him in life. But he didn't give me the idea that it defined him. He didn't rub it in my face or make me think he was just using it to get me in bed.

And that made me want to get in bed with him all the more.

Still, Carter was a stranger. And I didn't go home with strangers. I'd always had a theory that going home with strangers was asking for trouble. But when I thought about Ryan, I realized I hadn't known him all that well. I never would have thought he'd throw away something we'd worked on for so long…

For no reason at all.

And Carter… there was something about him that made him feel he wasn't a stranger at all. When we talked, it was like he understood me. And I hadn't had that with anyone.

Not with Ryan, and not with any of the guys I'd dated before.

Not even with my girlfriends, to be honest. Not like this. I'd always figured it was because I was an artist. A little different from everyone else. I hadn't expected anyone to truly understand me.

But somehow, it felt like Carter did.

And that wasn't something I wanted to let slip through my fingers.

So when he'd asked me if I wanted to go home with him, the only answer that had made logical sense was 'yes.'

We arrived at his apartment and he unlocked the door, letting me walk in first.

"Oh," I said when he flicked on the lights and I looked around. "This place doesn't look anything like my student apartment."

My place was a little dingy, with water damage on the ceiling, an oven I had to wedge shut with a broomstick, and a door I had to put my body weight behind to open or shut if I wanted to come or go.

Carter's place was neatly outfitted with modern designer furniture, and it had a clean, masculine scent.

Carter chuckled when I ogled the place.

"It's not much, but it's home."

"Are you kidding me?" I asked. "If this is your definition of 'not much,' I don't want to know what the rest of your life will look like when you're some crazy business mogul."

I shrugged out of my coat and Carter took it for me. A real gentleman.

He laughed. "You think I'm going to become a business mogul?"

"Oh, yes," I said.

He certainly looked the part. I was pretty sure he would be drop-dead gorgeous in a designer suit.

He was already jump-his-bones hot.

All he needed was to take that commanding air a step further and he was going to be everything.

He cupped my cheek, his face close to mine.

"You're staring," he mumbled, his lips so close to mine I could barely concentrate on the words he was speaking.

"You're distracting," I said.

I sounded like a fool. But he chuckled, and his voice was thick and smooth and it caressed my skin like honey.

When he kissed me, it was just as electric as it had been at the café when he'd pressed his lips against mine. But this time, it was different. There was so much more passion behind it. So much more lust. He pressed the length of his body against mine, and I could feel the bulge in his pants, proof of his growing interest in me.

And God, I wanted him. He was charming and handsome and confident—exactly the type of guy I never expected to end up with. And what was more, he wanted me, too.

I could feel it all the way down in his boxers, where his cock strained against his pants to get to me.

It was setting my body on fire, the way he ground himself against me. My stomach tightened. I was getting wet for him.

God, so wet.

Carter broke the kiss and looked at me.

"Can I get you something to drink?" he asked.

Was he serious? I didn't want anything to drink. Or to eat. Or anything that wasn't him naked and on top of me.

I blushed at myself, thinking things like this about a total stranger.

But then again, he didn't feel like a stranger to me.

I shook my head and kissed him, running my hands over his chest.

"I want to know where your bedroom is," I said.

Grab your copy of Boss's Secret Baby here!

Printed in Great Britain
by Amazon